Exiles from the Moor

Pauline Morphy

Published in 2011 by New Generation Publishing

Copyright © Pauline Morphy

First published in 1998 by New Millennium

ISBN: 978-1-9082484-8-0

First publication ISBN 1 85845 201 5, published in 1998

For Tamzin and Patrick, and in grateful memory of my parents and a ride on Exmoor, long ago, that began it all.

The cover shows Jess's painting of herself and Marmalade dreaming of their beloved Exmoor.

Chapter 1

The ponies checked, manes and tails streaming in the wind. The darkening sky, streaked by the silver rays of winter sunlight, made a fitting backcloth to their wild beauty. The leader whinnied and the glorious defiant sound carried through the herd like an electric pulse. Then they were off again, moving as one rippling body along the rim of the valley and wheeling to the left of a giant outcrop of rocks to begin the steep descent to the lush grass and clear, fast-flowing stream below.

Clutching a handful of mane and losing the damp reins in the springy hair, Jess knew her safety lay in going with her pony until she checked in unison with the herd. Down they plunged skirting large boulders, jumping small ones, skipping to the side of gorse bushes and sliding a little on the thick, purple carpet of heather and wortle. Exhilarated, yet a bit fearful, her breath caught by the wind, Jess clung on like a limpet. Then her pony's ears were coming closer and closer; she heard a high-pitched cry as she fell helplessly into a black engulfing void.

Her landing was soft and, although her legs were suspended, somehow, she was not being dragged. She felt safe but bewildered. The instant she realised where she was a crack of light appeared. It widened to reveal her mother standing in the doorway holding a tray. Light flooded the room and she saw she was lying with her head and shoulders on the floor and the rest of her caught up in the bedclothes.

"I heard a frightful scream," said her mother, Pam Redman. "Have you been in a fight?"

Jess giggled. "I've fallen off Marmalade. We were galloping downhill with the wild ponies."

Pam put the tray on the dressing stool and helped to untangle her.

"Good thing you kept hold of the reins," she said, laughing. "Marmalade is in the side paddock demolishing a hay net."

"Whatever time is it?" asked Jess, scrambling up and onto the bed.

"Oh, early-ish, not eight o'clock yet." Pam drew aside the heavy damask curtains, then poured two cups of tea and, handing one to Jess, sat down on the end of the bed.

"You're wearing your uniform," Jess exclaimed. "Do you have to?"

Pam looked down at the smart navy nurse's dress and considered for a moment.

"I don't know what Mrs Carey expects; so I thought it best to wear it."

"Did you get some sleep, Mum?"

"Yes, and so did Mrs Carey. In spite of having two strangers in the house she slept soundly until four o'clock then she needed something for her pain."

"Is she arthritic?" Jess asked, her voice not quite steady as she remembered her father's pain and discomfort.

"Yes, I'm afraid so. She's had it for so long, but I hope I can make her life a bit more comfortable. It's the illness I know most about." Her mother was silent for a few moments then stood up decisively. "I'll go and start breakfast in case Mrs Carey wakes up. D'you remember the way down to the kitchen?"

"Yes, turn right, right again and down the back stairs."

"That's it. You'll find yourself in a lobby with the kitchen door straight ahead."

Jess occasionally hugged the old-fashioned radiator for warmth while she dressed in the warmest clothes she could find. She looked around the large room comparing it unfavourably with her pretty bedroom at home. Pam had thoughtfully put some of Jess's own photographs and ornaments on the dressing table and her familiar books were in the bookcase but it still seemed an ugly, unfriendly room. She crossed to the window and looked out onto a shrubbery that filled the vee formed by the drive dividing, one part continuing to the front of the house and the other to the garages and stables. Beyond the shrubbery in a paddock beside the drive was a familiar mouse-brown shape, totally absorbed, eating. Cheering up, Jess picked up the tea tray and found her way down to the lobby. There, the sight of her saddle and bridle on a wooden horse and her tack box nearby raised her spirits even higher.

The kitchen was warm and welcoming. Pam stood by the Aga, frying bacon, mushrooms and tomatoes. She smiled at Jess and said, "There's fresh tea in the pot."

"Thanks." Jess helped herself and topped up her mother's cup. "Is all that for me?"

Pam tipped the contents of the pan onto a large oval plate and laughed.

"For both of us, I hope. Mrs Carey will ring when she's ready for hers, just scrambled eggs and coffee."

They sat at a large scrubbed table and Jess glanced around the room while they ate. It was old-fashioned with solid looking cupboards and deep drawers with brass handles, a polished red tiled floor and, suspended from the ceiling, a rack on which tea towels were drying in the heat from the Aga.

"I like this room," she said. "I'm sure I'll want to spend more time here than in my bedroom."

"You'll like the little sitting-room next door," Pam replied, looking pleased. "It's so pretty and comfortable. I think the house must have been lovely years ago but the main rooms are all under dust sheets."

"I don't like the dark, old furniture in my bedroom," Jess said. "What's Mrs Carey's room like?"

"Lovely, you'll see it soon."

"Oh no, when do I have to meet her?"

"Today, at three-o'clock. She wants you to have tea with her. Now, don't look like that, I'm sure you'll like her."

"Mum, I'll be so nervous I'll spill my tea, or say something I shouldn't."

"Don't be silly. She isn't half as formidable as your Great Aunt Elizabeth and you cope with her."

"Shall I have to wear a dress?"

"Well maybe, for the first visit."

Jess looked so horrified that Pam conceded hastily, "Well at least put on a skirt and jersey - clean ones, and do brush your hair. Now what about the rest of the day? How about exploring the village?"

The kitchen door opened and a tall, red-cheeked woman came in carrying a bulging string bag and a bunch of daffodils. Pam stood up extending a hand and introducing Jess, who suddenly remembered her manners and jumped up to shake hands with Mrs Mundy, the daily housekeeper.

"Call me Maggie," she invited. "Everyone else does." She gave a throaty chuckle, put the flowers on the draining board and rummaged in the bag extracting a red apple.

"There duck, for your little pony."

"Oh thanks, that's really kind." Jess beamed at her. "Did you see her by the drive?"

"I did. She gave my bike an old-fashioned look. Don't expect she sees much traffic where she comes from."

Jess caught her mother's eye and looked away hastily. She was going to like Maggie.

"How's Mrs Carey?" Maggie asked, divesting herself of her coat and scarf, revealing a mop of springy grey hair as thick as wire wool.

"She's had quite a good night. I'll go up in a minute in case she's ready for her breakfast."

As if on cue, Mrs Carey's bell rang.

"That'll be for breakfast now," said Maggie. "You finish yours and let me take hers up. You must be worn out."

"I'm not really, although I must admit I mainly dozed. I had half an ear open in case she rang."

"Well, I'll go and say `Hello' and get my orders," Maggie said and chuckled as she picked up Mrs Carey's tray. "It's us who needs lifts," she said, "not breakfast trays."

"Mum, she's lovely," said Jess as the kitchen door closed.

"I think so too. She's worked here for years and remembers Mrs Carey's son who died really young. I heard all about her when I came for the interview. She and Mrs Carey are more like old friends than employer and employee."

"Mum, I'll wash up, I promise, but I want to go out to Marmalade first."

"That's all right. Don't forget the apple."

Jess quartered the apple then cut it into thin slices. She collected her coat and a headcollar and went out into the yard to be hit by an icy blast of wind that took her breath away. Mrs Munday's bike lay on its side so she picked it up and leaned it against the stable wall on the sheltered side of the yard. Her feet scrunched on the gravel and, recognising her step, Marmalade called with her deep distinctive whinny.

Jess sank her fingers into the pony's dense coat and rubbed her cheek against her great wayward mane. Munching her apple, Marmalade stood with patient contentment as Jess hugged her a dozen times, then she took a good thirty minutes brushing mud off her. She loved being close to the pony, revelling in the smell of her and the warmth that seemed to radiate from her winter coat. Marmalade flicked her ears whenever Jess spoke and made snuffly noises in response.

Carrying her tack out through the back door Jess met Maggie coming back from emptying a waste bin.

"Bring her into the yard, duck. You'll both be warmer round here. Sam will probably let you use the stable, which will make it easier for you, and your little pony will enjoy some company."

She went indoors leaving Jess puzzling over her last remark. She understood Mrs Carey had ridden all her life and she and her late husband had kept several hunters, but there were no signs of horses being around any more. She looked at the huge stable door and imagined high-sided loose boxes with a gullied passage down the centre. She had already tried the door and found it locked.

Maggie had directed Jess to a bridleway that started at the end of the drive, skirted the paddocks then curved away from The Elms, westwards. Alert to every unfamiliar sight and sound, Marmalade walked out eagerly while Jess looked around critically at the neat, gentle countryside. The bridleway joined a farm track that ran sharply back leftwards, almost parallel to the way she had come, and ahead into a farmyard.

She sat pondering which way to go. A tractor came along the track and stopped a few yards away. The driver switched off the engine and called,

"Are you lost?"

He looked a bit older than Jess and had a pleasant, friendly face.

"I'm trying to follow the bridle-path."

The boy jumped down from the cab and, pulling the yard gate away from the wall and across the entrance, pointed to a blue arrow painted on the top bar now facing her.

"Sorry," He called. "I renewed it recently and put it there instead of on the gate post. Now, you can only see it when the gate's shut, which it never is. I s'pose I'd better change it or we'll have the Rights of Way officer on to us, not to mention half the Pony Club." He pushed the gate back against the wall.

Jess thanked him and asked if he lived on the farm. He told her it was his dad's farm and then, as he swung himself up into the cab, said, "I s'pose you're from The Elms?"

Surprised, Jess said that she was and wanted to ask him how he knew but he started the engine and, grinning broadly, waved her on through the yard ahead of him. On the far side of the very tidy yard, the track turned at a right angle towards a big farmhouse, and on the left, a smaller path followed the field boundary. Jess and Marmalade went that way.

The sun appeared from behind a pewter-coloured cloud but there was little warmth in it. The hedge leaves were still tightly furled and just a few brave celandines beamed up from the hedge bottom.

"Let's have a canter," Jess suggested gathering the pony together, but the word 'canter' was enough for Marmalade.

After a few hundred yards the path narrowed and meandered so, afraid of meeting walkers or other riders, Jess told Marmalade to "Steady - steady," while gently increasing the rein contact and the pressure with her legs. Responsive to the lightest touch as she had never been tugged by her rider, the mare slowed immediately and Jess pecked onto her neck. She gave the pony a hug before righting herself and told her she had an excellent mouth.

Ahead was a lane that they followed eastwards until they arrived at The Elms. Jess dismounted in the drive and led Marmalade towards the stable yard, but at the entrance she stopped abruptly, snorting, head high, eyes rolling and ears pricked.

"What is it? What's up, old girl?"

Jess stroked her neck and gently urged her forward but she would not budge. For several minutes they stood, Jess straining her ears to hear whatever it was that had caused her to freeze. Gradually the pony relaxed and Jess was able to lead her on.

Pam came out with a bowl of sliced carrots, which took all Marmalade's attention. Jess described her behaviour and Pam suggested she was expressing natural suspicion and caution at being in a strange place. Jess was not convinced and said she'd heard that horses were particularly aware of the supernatural.

Pam laughed. "Perhaps there are ghosts of long-dead horses around."

As she disappeared through the back door, Jess caught a whiff of stew and felt ravenous. She untacked swiftly, passed the dandy brush over the saddle mark then led Marmalade back to her paddock. With satisfaction she watched her slowly crumple her forelegs, slump onto her right shoulder then fling all four legs in the air. Only when she was sure that she was as muddy as she could be did she clamber to her feet with a satisfied snort.

Jess was reprieved: Mrs Carey was feeling very tired and had decided to postpone their meeting for twenty-four hours. Jess's relief was profound, but what was she to do instead? Too restless to immerse herself in drawing, reading or watching television, she needed a practical task; so decided to give her tack a thorough clean. She started by undoing every strap and testing the buckles and stitching for safety. Once the leather was clean she used Silvo on all the metal parts, then reassembled the bridle examining the holes for blocking saddle soap. She then cleaned and polished her saddle until it gleamed like a horse chestnut. Finally, she scrubbed out her tack box and cleaned the brushes.

Where on earth was her mother? She'd been with Mrs Carey for hours. She'd snatched twenty minutes for lunch, then disappeared upstairs again to meet the doctor.

Resentfully, she thought of the American zoologist who was living in her home, studying the wildlife on the moor. He'd seemed a nice enough man but had he the wit to realise he was living in the best place on Earth?

She felt tears pricking her eyelids as she wondered for the millionth time why her father had to die. A knock on the back door interrupted her sad and angry thoughts. A merry-faced, pink-cheeked boy about her own age was standing in the yard beside a coloured pony.

"Hi, I'm Adam Barnes," he announced. "D'you want to come riding? You are the girl Tom Latcham saw this morning, aren't you?"

Feeling overwhelmed Jess said she didn't know, but she had seen a boy on a tractor and he seemed to know who she was.

"That's right, that's Tom so it must have been you. I've just come through his yard. I thought you might want someone to ride with."

Jess's thoughts raced. She'd be at least half-an-hour getting Marmalade clean and it was nearly five and a dark afternoon.

"I don't mean now," Adam said. "I'm on my way home. Maybe tomorrow if Dad doesn't find me too many chores to do."

Jess smiled her relief. "Gosh yes. Look, can you stay for a drink? I can't put your pony in the stable 'cause it's locked, but I can lend you a head collar. Will he stay tied up?"

"Oh he'll stay," Adam said.

Jess handed him Marmalade's head collar, then showed him a ring in the wall beside the big stable door. Watching him buckle the head collar over his pony's bridle she started to worry. Should she have invited a stranger into Mrs Carey's house?

"Won't he be cold?" she asked.

Adam laughed. "No, he's really tough. We had quite a slow ride so he's hardly sweating."

A throaty whinny reminded Jess that Marmalade was just a few yards away. The gelding lifted his head and answered politely.

"Will he pull away and try to reach Marmalade?"

"No, he'll be fine. We saw your pony by the drive. She's very friendly. I like her name; it's a bit like our junior dog's - Marmite."

Jess grinned. "I like that. What's your pony called?"

"Pied Piper but Pie for short - not very original but it seems right for him."

Jess led the way indoors. "Tea, coffee, cocoa, or something cold?" she offered taking two mugs from the dresser.

"Tea, please." Adam unfastened and removed his hard hat revealing thick, fair hair, then unzipped his blue anorak worn over a Pony Club sweatshirt.

Jess put the biscuit tin on the table, inviting him to help himself. He carefully chose a chocolate cream.

"Have several," Jess suggested and he beamed.

"What's the old lady, Mrs Carey, like? We never see her."

"I haven't met her yet. I was going to have tea with her today but she wasn't up to it. Mum likes her and, I suppose, she must be quite nice to let me bring Marmalade."

Adam said, "We know Mrs Munday. She's really nice. Mum saw her last week in the post office and heard all about you coming here. Now everyone will know about you in this little place."

How could he call Berrywood a `little place'? Maggie had told her it had a hotel, a pub, a garage and two shops. To Jess that meant a town.

"How long have you lived here, Adam?"

"About four years. We used to live in St Albans but Dad grew up on a farm and wanted a proper country practice."

"Is your dad a doctor?"

"No, a vet. What about yours? Has he come to Surrey with you?"

Jess was filling the teapot. She swallowed hard then, in a tight voice, replied, "Dad died just over eight months ago. He had heart trouble and arthritis for ages. We've let our cottage and come here, so we don't have to sell it."

Staring hard at the table, Adam said, "Sorry, I shouldn't have asked."

Jess put a mug of tea in front of him and sat down opposite. "It's okay. Help yourself to sugar."

Adam did so, spooning in two cubes.

"Tell me about your pony. He looks big compared with Marmalade."

Adam relaxed. "He's 13.2 and rising eight. Dad found him tethered on a grass verge when he was a yearling. He wasn't quite an R.S.P.C.A. case but Dad was sure he'd have a miserable life. He managed to persuade the owner to sell him and he was kept at a riding school until we came here. He's done quite well in Coloured Pony Show Classes and he's an ace jumper. He does everything at Pony Club. Are you a member?"

"No. We lived too far from most of the rallies. I always ride alone." Instantly she regretted her words and quickly added, "I mean there weren't any children nearby to ride with."

Adam said, "My sister's away staying with a friend from our old school, but I know she'll want to ride with you. She gets really fed up being with her little brother."

"How much older is she?" Jess reckoned Adam was about eleven – her age.

"Ten minutes," said Adam, grinning. "We're twins. Susan's all right, I s'pose – well, most of the time. Mum says she'll either be a teacher or a Member of Parliament 'cause she likes telling people what to do."

"What's her pony like?"

"Brilliant. Another of Dad's finds. She was going for meat at the horse sales. She's Arab crossed with New Forest and really good-looking. She can be a bit fiery and is really competitive - a bit like Susan - well, not the good-looking bit."

To Jess's amusement he blushed. She already liked this boy who was so easy to talk to.

"Where d'you go to school?"

"The local comprehensive. Is that where you're going?"

Jess beamed. "Yes, what's it like?"

Adam shrugged. "All right, I s'pose, as schools go. They're good on music. I'm in the orchestra. Quite a lot of people ride and belong to the Pony Club. You'll join, won't you? There's a rally before term starts."

"Do they have very smart ponies?"

Adam considered this for a moment. "Pretty mixed. Some like Pie and Tara and some kept up like hunters. There are quite a lot of show ponies. I s'pose we're quite a competitive branch but we're lucky as we've an indoor and outdoor school we can use and a cross-country course."

"Gosh, it will all be a bit new to me," Jess admitted. "Usually, we just go for rides across the moor, jumping everything possible as Marmalade loves jumping and...."

"The D.C. will love you then," interrupted Adam. "She hunts three days a week so thinks jumping's everything."

Jess offered Adam more tea but he declined politely and said he ought to go as it would soon be dark.

"Thanks anyway." He reached for his hat. "Oh, and thanks for the - biscuits." He looked slightly abashed; Jess noticed the tin was empty and so was the sugar bowl.

"How far d'you have to go?" Jess asked, getting up.

Adam fastened his chinstrap and zipped his anorak. "About half a mile. We're down the left-hand lane just before the village."

Jess collected Marmalade's hay net from a shed to the left of the stable block.

"Why can't you use the stable?" Adam said. "We've never seen horses around here so it's probably been empty for years. Seems a waste."

"I expect I'll be able to use it. Mrs Munday said something about it this morning."

Adam gently tightened the girth and pulled the stirrups down. "I don't suppose an Exmoor needs a stable," he commented. "Dad says they're the most ancient breed in Britain. Didn't their ancestors survive the Ice Age?"

"Yes." Jess was surprised and pleased. "They're a rare breed. Exmoor was an army training area in the Second World War and lots of ponies were killed."

"By accident I hope!" said Adam, shocked. He pulled a grubby pair of gloves out of his pocket then, simultaneously with Jess, stared at Pie. Suddenly the pony had gone rigid, his head towards the stable with one ear back, listening intently.

"How odd," Jess exclaimed. "Marmalade did that this morning as if she'd heard or seen something that I didn't."

Adam spoke to Pie and stroked his neck but it was a few moments before the pony relaxed and lowered his muzzle into his master's hand. Jess grinned, hearing the crunch of a sugar cube.

"Horses are very psychic, like dogs," Adam said, confidently. He mounted Pie lightly and squeezed him forward. Jess walked alongside carrying the net that she tied to the paddock gate. Marmalade whinnied, more interested in Pie than her hay. Adam laughed at her muddy state and said it was a clever way of keeping warm.

"The gate isn't locked," he commented suddenly.

Surprised, Jess asked, "Why d'you think it should be? We never lock the gates at home."

"Yes, but this isn't Exmoor. We're a bit too close to London here. Gangs come out to the countryside and steal anything they can grab - sheep, calves, horses, tack - anything! We padlock all our gates and our ponies are freeze-branded."

"Marmalade has her own special brand," Jess said, a little defensively. She didn't want to be thought a careless owner so, at the earliest opportunity, she'd buy a stout chain and padlock. What a dreadful, lawless place they'd come to!

"See you soon," called Adam. He trotted Pie smartly along the drive accompanied by Marmalade until the paddock fence curved away, so she then hurried back to her hay net.

Watching her eating Jess went over Adam's words and felt uneasy. She shivered suddenly and violently and, giving Marmalade a parting pat, went indoors.

"At last! I was wondering when I'd next see you," Jess's tone was reproachful. Her mother was sitting in a rocking chair, stretching her legs towards the Aga and attempting to stifle a yawn.

"You look really tired," Jess told her. "Has Mrs Carey been giving you a hard time?"

With a tiny note of reproof Pam replied, "Mrs Carey's been having a hard time from pain and discomfort. She's sleeping at last." She smiled at Jess, looking brighter than she felt.

"What have you been doing?"

Jess described Adam's visit and was relieved that her mother approved of her inviting him indoors. When she reached the bit about Pie freezing like a statue, the piercing ring of Mrs Carey's bell made them both jump. With a resigned sigh Pam got up and left the room.

Jess, cut off at the intriguing part of her story, was left with the unease she had felt earlier. Putting on a coat, she went to check Marmalade and, as she closed the back door, she thought a shadowy figure moved away to her right. With her hand still on the door handle she looked over her shoulder but saw only the dark shapes of bushes and the kitchen-garden wall. There was no moon to cast mysterious shadows, so perhaps it was just her imagination. She walked to the edge of the yard and peered into the dark garden, determined to be brave. If there were bad people around she had a duty to find out, particularly after Adam's warning. She crossed the cobbles, reassured by the sound her boots made, and the pool of light from the kitchen window lighting her way to the drive.

Marmalade whickered a greeting and nudged her arm so she dug deep into her pockets and found a broken polo mint and some bread crumbs. Marmalade licked her hand clean then returned to her net.

Resolving to buy a padlock and chain tomorrow without fail, Jess returned indoors, carefully turning the big key and shooting the bolts on the back door.

Chapter 2

Jess tentatively knocked on Mrs Carey's door. A clear voice called, "Come in."

Doing as she was told, Jess entered a warm, bright room that was like a bowl of pink and cream roses. A frail-looking woman sat on a small sofa, holding out thin trembling hands sparkling with rings that were too loose. She was the prettiest old lady Jess had ever seen. Her hair was pure white and abundant, and her brilliant violet eyes scrutinised Jess with an unnerving intensity. After shaking hands and inviting her to sit down she smiled and said, "You are so like a photograph your mother showed me of your late father - the same chestnut hair and brown eyes. Lucky girl."

Jess blushed but was pleased with the compliment. Mrs Carey continued, "I hear you are an artist, so you take after him in that way also."

Jess nodded, swallowing hard. She didn't want to discuss her father with a stranger.

"I hope you are a quiet child. I couldn't cope with anyone shouting and rushing around."

Affronted, Jess replied, "I expect I did a bit when I was little."

"Well, I'm sure you're well-behaved. I have no contact with children now and one gets such a bad impression from the television. However, you ride and that's a good thing. I suppose you belong to the Pony Club?"

"Um... No, the rallies were all so far away."

"What a pity. I was the District Commissioner for many years. It's essential training and a perfect way of making friends. I do advise you to join."

Jess looked away from the unwavering gaze. Why did grown-ups, even complete strangers, believe they always had a right to tell children what to do?

"I understand you're going to a the local school but I would have thought a boarding school would have been more suitable. As an only child you must get very lonely."

Jess now met Mrs Carey's gaze and firmly replied, "No, I like being on my own. Anyway, I've a best friend – Liz, near Porlock."

"Ah, but that isn't here. You'll need local friends. I'm not sure where you'll find them."

"I've met two boys already," Jess began, but Mrs Carey seemed not to be listening.

"You'll find it all so different here; no moor on which to ride, just bridle-paths and lanes full of ill-mannered motorists."

"Marmalade is brilliant in traffic," Jess interposed. "We made sure it was part of her schooling."

"Good. It will be put to the test. You understand you'll have to look after your pony yourself. Your mother will be fully occupied looking after me."

Jess flushed. "I always look after Marmalade. She doesn't need a lot of looking-after. She hates being in a stable and always lives out. The hardest part is getting the mud off..."

Suddenly, Mrs Carey laughed and her expression changed completely. She looked kind, and even prettier.

"I'm picturing her coated with mud. Tell me about her. Has she settled in?"

Jess relaxed a little. "Yes, I think so. She looks as she always does; so I suppose she's happy. She really enjoyed the ride but – perhaps, she misses the views..."

"How do you mean?"

"Well, she has small paddocks bordered by low stone walls and she can see for miles, even to the sea but, here, she can only see hedges."

"Ah... Yes, she probably does miss her panoramic views."

Afraid her criticism may have appeared rude, Jess said, "I think she really only cares about food and she has plenty here."

To her relief Mrs Carey chuckled. "What's her name? Your mother did tell me but my memory is poor nowadays."

"Marmalade."

"Ah yes, I like it. How did the name come about?"

Jess took a deep breath. "She was an orange colour when she was born, and Daddy told me a story about Mary, Queen of Scots, only before that - when she was married to the little French King. One day she was ill and her cook was very worried and wanted to make something special for her. He made a jelly of oranges and lemons and was saying, `Marie est Malade', over and over again. That means `Mary is ill,' and it became `Marmalade', and Mary was the name of Marmalade's dam and she was very sick when we got her..."

Her breath ran out. Pink faced she stared at her tightly clasped hands wondering what on earth Mrs Carey was thinking of her.

"That's a lovely story and why should it not be true? Many of these old tales are. So, Marmalade has small paddocks at home and, no doubt, you have to keep them clean?"

"Oh yes." Jess was surprised at the question. "I pick up droppings several times a week"

"My gardener comes only twice a week so he couldn't keep the paddocks clean. We mustn't increase his workload. Nowadays, good gardeners are like gold dust."

There was a long pause. The gentle ticking of a clock was the only sound in the room except, perhaps, Jess's breathing. She longed for her mother or Maggie to appear. The old lady had closed her eyes. Was she asleep?

"My own experience is limited to hunters."

Jess started. Once again she was under the scrutiny of those bright violet eyes; Mrs Carey was wide-awake.

"We always bred our own. They're all here." She waved her hand indicating framed photographs almost covering one wall, then asked Jess to hand her one that was on the sofa table. Taking it in both painfully twisted hands she held it very close to her face.

"Yes, this is the one." She turned the glass towards Jess and said, "My last remaining hunter. Isn't she beautiful?"

The mare was indeed beautiful. She looked full of quality, with perfect conformation, a glossy, dark brown coat and fine, intelligent head. Her rider was sitting side-saddle wearing hunting dress.

"Is that you, Mrs Carey? Did you always ride side-saddle?"

"Yes, dear, and no. My mother insisted I learnt both ways. That photograph was taken at a show almost fourteen years ago and, now, my dear Sonata is twenty although you wouldn't think so to see her." She laid the photograph on the sofa.

"Now, my dear, will you be kind enough to help me up. If we go to the window you'll have a surprise."

As she spoke a pretty clock in a glass cover chimed the half hour. Jess positioned herself so that Mrs Carey could use her arm for support. Seeing her taut, controlled expression and slow movements, punctuated by two rests between sofa and window, Jess felt sad. An image of her father's pain and physical limitations filled her mind for a moment.

Reaching the window Mrs Carey sank down on a strategically placed chair and, a little breathlessly, said, "My lovely Sonata. Whenever I'm feeling well enough she arrives at three-thirty so I can see her and know she is fine."

In front of them was a view of the curving drive, the circular flowerbed with its small pond and fountain, and on its far side stood a horse. Holding it was a very old man, who seemed to be doing his best to stand to attention. A navy blue rug largely concealed the horse but even so it was obvious that she was pitifully thin. Her neck hung down as if the head on the end was too heavy for its support, and she stood on widely splayed legs, gently swaying from side to side. If she lifted a foot she would totter and fall, Jess thought, too appalled to speak.

"It nearly breaks my heart that I can hardly see her - just a horse-shaped blur. My eyes are so weak, but Sam gives me a regular bulletin and he is such an old and trusted friend."

Jess realised a response was expected. She felt swift panic rising in her throat and then, at last, finding her words she sounded croaky with emotion. "She must have been wonderful when she was young."

"Oh, indeed she was. We won the Ladies' Hunter class at Windsor and at several county shows. She was as bold as she was beautiful. I see her now, in my mind's eye, as she was then and, really, I don't suppose she's very different."

What could Jess reply? She realised Mrs Carey had no idea of the present condition of the old mare and from what she could see of the groom, Sam, it seemed his condition was little better. He slowly lifted a hand in salute and the pair of them tottered across the drive and out of sight around the corner of the house.

The next half hour was like a nightmare for Jess. She supposed she managed to pour the tea, brought in by Pam, pass plates and respond adequately to Mrs Carey's chatter, while her mind was filled with the picture of the pathetic old mare and the last glimpse of her narrow quarters and stringy tail.

Free at last, she put the tea things on the draining board while describing the awful scene to her mother. Looking worried and thoughtful, Pam told her that Sam was long retired but had volunteered to look after the mare because he had helped at her birth and adored her. He had a tiny cottage at the edge of Mrs Carey's land on the village side and came in at least twice a day to look after the mare.

"When did you learn all this, Mum?" Jess demanded.

"Only this morning from Maggie. I was sworn to secrecy so as not to spoil your surprise."

"But how can Maggie bear it? She loves animals."

"I wonder if she even knows the state the mare is in. She arrives after Sam goes home and leaves before he returns. Also, she doesn't know anything about horses, although her daughter used to ride and show the hunters for Mrs Carey."

At that moment Mrs Carey's bell rang. Giving Jess a sympathetic squeeze, Pam hurried out of the room and, dropping the tea towel, Jess almost ran out to the yard and with a thumping heart, tried the stable door. To her surprise it opened and cautiously she peered into gloom. It was just as she had visualised; high-sided boxes separated by a concrete passage. There was a strong smell of dusty hay and ammonia.

Nervously, Jess called, "Hello, is anyone there?"

There was no reply. Jess pushed the door wide open and took a step inside. She called again, a little louder, and this time she heard a rustling sound to her right and slow, shuffling footsteps.

"Who's that?" The voice was quavery.

"Jess Redman, my mother's the new nurse here."

"Ah - want to see the mare?"

"Please." The relief made her legs quite wobbly as she went down the passageway to the last box on the left. Sam opened the door and stood aside to allow her in, and there was the old mare, head hanging down and, facing the wall, she showed no flicker of interest in her visitor.

"Lovely mare, that. Best we ever bred and we had some beauties."

There was love and pride in his voice. Jess's throat felt tight as she quietly went up to the mare's head and rubbed her behind her ears. Almost imperceptibly she moved the ear nearest to Jess. As Sam had walked, or tottered, away, Jess risked slipping her hand under the rug and felt the bony shoulder and hoop-like ribs. She shuddered.

Sam returned carrying a bucket. Water slopped from it onto the meagre straw bed.

"Oh, let me help," Jess said, moving towards him but Sam shook his head and, in a less friendly tone, told her he could manage. With difficulty he placed the bucket in the corner bracket.

"Would she like some company, d'you think?" Jess asked. "I could put my pony next to her sometimes; so they could get used to each other and go out in the paddock together on warm days."

She was amazed at her boldness. Sam took some while considering this then, to her surprise, he said, "We might try them together - when the warm weather comes. Best leave her now, so she'll eat."

Jess doubted his words but left the box and watched him reach painfully to a switch on the wall. Only then did she realise there was a light on. It was a single bulb hanging high above them and so festooned with dusty cobwebs that its extinction hardly mattered. She followed Sam outside and watched him carefully lock the door. She expected he would pocket the key but he put it in a crack between loose bricks in the stable wall.

"Valuable mare that," he said. "Can't take any chances nowadays."

"Yes, of course. Thank you for showing her to me."

"That's all right. G'night."

Sam went slowly across the yard and disappeared down a path leading through the kitchen garden to his cottage. Jess stood motionless listening to the diminishing footsteps. A memory from last evening flashed into her mind; it was Sam's disappearing figure she had seen and not a ghost or trick of her imagination.

Satisfied he had really gone she turned back to the stable and felt for the hidden key. As her fingers closed over it she was aware of a strange mixture of guilt and excitement. Cautiously, as if she thought she might be overheard, she turned the key in the lock, pushed open the heavy door and went along the passageway. She switched on the light and entered the box but, again, there was no response from Sonata. Very quietly and gently, Jess removed her rug and was shocked by the gaunt outline. She felt her high backbone and hollows inside her flanks and, as the mare flinched beneath her touch, she realised she had rug sores. She put the rug back and stroked Sonata's head, talking to her all the time.

Careful to leave everything as she had found it, she hurried indoors to find the kitchen empty. She washed her hands then, in frustration and anxiety, she paced the floor willing her mother to appear. To calm herself she listened to the radio. At last Pam arrived. She stopped in the doorway, dismayed at Jess's expression.

"You've seen the old mare?"

"Yes, Sam let me go inside. Mum, she's worse than I thought. She's really like a toast rack and has great rub marks on her back. Do come and see her... We'll need a torch to see her properly."

Pam hesitated then, with a glance at the clock said, "I can risk ten minutes. There's a flash lamp in the lobby."

They stood looking at Sonata for several minutes not saying a word and then Pam asked,

"Have you seen her eat or drink anything?"

"No, the hay hasn't been touched." She shone the lamp into the bucket. "I think she's had a drink."

"Hmm, I imagine her teeth are too long to allow her to chew properly." Pam stroked the thin neck.

"What can we do, Mum? She really is starving, isn't she?"

"Yes, I'm afraid so. Cover her up now and we'll go indoors and try to work something out."

Jess left Sonata still standing with her head hanging listlessly. She washed her hands at the kitchen sink and put the kettle on as Pam requested.

"If nothing else she can have a little warm gruel. She might just be tempted by it."

"What is it, Mum?"

"Just a handful of flour dissolved in warm water. It's old-fashioned but we used to give it to the hunters after a hard day and they loved it."

Jess didn't doubt the wisdom of her mother's advice. She had worked with horses and passed some B.H.S. exams before taking up nursing.

"We can try soaking the hay to soften it a bit but there's nothing else we can do tonight. We'll have to think how we can explain all this to Mrs Carey without upsetting her too much."

"Mum, the feelings of an old lady, who is waited on day and night, can't be more important than a poor starving horse!"

Her mother passed her a mug of tea and refilled the kettle.

"Darling, you surely know me better than that, but Mrs Carey is Sonata's owner; she can decide what happens to her."

"How long will it take to talk to her, Mum? We can't leave the old mare suffering much longer. Why don't we ring Adam's father as he's the nearest vet?"

Pam sat down, rested her forehead in her hands briefly then, pushing back her fair hair, smiled wearily. "Every horse above a certain age needs a yearly check-up, so that's the way we'll approach this."

"And if it doesn't work?"

Pam was silent for a second. "Then - drastic measures, I promise. A few more days won't affect Sonata too much so try to be patient. Once Sam's been we'll soak her hay and give her gruel at night, and spend time with her between his visits. That's more than she's had for years."

She looked in the cupboards for some flour. In a matter-of-fact voice, she asked, "How did you get on with Mrs Carey? It must have been harder for you once you'd seen Sonata."

Jess looked sharply at her mother, suspicious of the too casual tone and bland expression. Bluntly, she said, "She didn't want me to come here, did she?"

Pam hesitated. "She was apprehensive. She'd have preferred a nurse without ties."

"So why are we here?" Jess's tone was challenging.

Pam poured more tea before replying. "She took to me. She'd interviewed several people but hadn't particularly liked any of them. I was fairly - uncertain, but she was so pleasant to me, and Maggie was lovely. She did say rather a lot about the merits of boarding schools and I was close to refusing the job, then Maggie told me about the local school which sounded good. There was more than adequate grazing for Marmalade and, apparently, lots of horsy children in the neighbourhood. Well - I began to like the idea more and more..."

"But she'd rather I wasn't here?"

Pam sighed. "I'm not sure - honestly. She thinks you're well-mannered and seem sensible, and you care about your pony..."

"Isn't that enough?"

"Yes - yes, I expect it is."

There was a strained silence then, in a tight voice, Jess said, "I won't go away to school. I'll never, ever leave Marmalade."

Pam looked at her, a hurt expression in her eyes. "Jess, the question will never arise. Mrs Carey wanted me to take the job; so she had to accept that with me came you and with you came Marmalade - a sort of package deal."

Jess could not help grinning.

"Come on now," said Pam. "We'll make the gruel for Sonata and tuck her up. Try to be patient, darling. I'm sure we'll all shake down together quite comfortably, but it will take time."

Privately, Jess thought she had no choice but to 'shake down'. She collected their coats from the lobby and, thrusting her hands in her pockets, her fingers closed over the key to the padlock that now secured Marmalade's gate. A reminder of the hazards of living in 'civilised' Surrey!

Jess did not sleep well. She had disturbing dreams all about Sonata. At breakfast her mother was preoccupied, worrying about Mrs Carey, who had also had a bad night. Mrs Munday's arrival was a relief. Jess poured out her story in a rush, which caused Maggie to sit down in the nearest chair, shocked at what she was hearing.

"How could I allow it to happen? Only yards from my kitchen, the old mare starving to death..."

"It's not your fault," said Jess, hastily. "Sam's the groom and you hardly see him and her."

But Maggie continued to be hard on herself. She insisted on inspecting Sonata, then helped Jess to carry gruel to her. She agreed that something had to be done and careful tactics had to be discussed.

They saw little of Pam who joined them briefly for lunch then hurried back upstairs. Sensing how helpless and frustrated Jess was feeling Maggie urged her to go for a ride.

"There's a look of snow about," she warned. "You get out while you can."

"Surely not!" Jess exclaimed. "It's spring."

"Makes no odds," Maggie said, grimly. "I can remember sunshine at Easter and snow in May – that was before your mum was even born."

An hour and a half and a refreshing, brisk ride later, Jess was tying a bulging hay net high up on the top bar of Marmalade's gate, when she was attracted by the sound of hoof beats on the bridle-path. She gave the net a testing tug, slipped Marmalade's head collar off and stood listening intently. The light was poor but she could make out the shapes of two ponies and riders beyond the far fence and the winter - thinned hedge. Hoping that one of them was Adam she was about to call out and run across the paddock when a high-pitched girl's voice reached her straining ears.

"Oh look! Whatever is it?"

A similar voice suggested, "It's a hearth rug," and tailed off in fits of laughter.

Marmalade, always a friendly pony, whinnied and trotted over to the fence.

"Would you ride it?" asked the first voice. "Or just sit on it?"

"I know what it is," said the second voice. "It's a gnu!" This set them both off into shrieks of laughter and then they began to sing. "I'm a gnu, I'm a gnu, I'm the g'nicest work of g'nature in the zoo," followed by more shrieks

But Jess was not laughing. Clenching her fists, she strode across the paddock crying: "Stop it, you silly little beasts! Can't you recognise an Exmoor pony when you see one?"

There was silence, then a scurrying noise as they urged their ponies into trot; their unrestrained laughter carried back to Jess with snatches of: "I'm not a hartebeest, I'm a gnu. G'no, g'no, g'no, I'm a gnu..."

The song was one of many that Jess's father used to sing to her when she was tiny. He made funny faces and they laughed together; now Jess couldn't even smile.

Marmalade, apparently unconcerned, ambled over and nudged her gently. Jess flung her arms around her neck, telling her she was the most wonderful and beautiful pony in the World and, not doubting her, Marmalade gave a long, satisfied sigh.

Chapter 3

Jess awoke to find snow had fallen as predicted by Maggie. Gasping at the coldness of the air she stuffed hay into a net and hurried to feed Marmalade who had already dug down to find grass. The pony whinnied and put a snowy muzzle against Jess's cheek.

"I don't like frozen kisses," Jess told her, dusting her face.

The ice on the trough was too thick to be broken with a stick so Jess went to fetch some hot water. She narrowly missed colliding with a young postman who seemed very agitated.

"It's the old man in the cottage …" he paused, gasping for breath. "He's lying on the path - by his back door. He's not moving – unconscious, I think… "

Jess had opened the kitchen door and was calling her mother before he had finished speaking. Straight away Pam telephoned for an ambulance, instructed Jess to listen for Mrs Carey's bell and was off down the path with the postman at her heels. The ambulance arrived within twenty minutes and with gentle deftness Sam was lifted into it. Then Pam checked everything was secure in the cottage before she, Jess and the postman, returned to the kitchen to warm themselves with tea, eggs and bacon.

Listening to the adults speculating on what might have happened to Sam if there hadn't been a letter for him, Jess suddenly leapt up, crying, "The old mare – oh, how awful."

In the stable she looked for suitable food for Sonata. Marmalade's pony nuts would be indigestible but, perhaps, a little damp, molassed chaff would be easier to eat than hay. Sonata showed no interest in it. Jess broke up a whole bale of straw to top up her bed. It seemed to be the last one.

She waited impatiently for her mother to come down from breaking the news to Mrs Carey. What would happen to Sonata now? Pam suspected Sam had suffered a stroke. As the implication of this dawned on Jess she flushed, wondering if it was very wicked to feel relief for the old mare mixed up with concern for poor Sam. There was no escaping the fact that the accident had probably solved the problem of Sonata's welfare.

She heard the back door open and found Maggie scraping snow from her boots. In dismay she listened to Jess's story while draping her damp scarf and gloves on the Aga rail.

"Has anyone told Sam's daughter, Jenny? She lives a bit north of London."

Jess said she didn't know as her mother was still with Mrs Carey.

"Well, Mrs C will ring I expect, poor soul. Nice woman, his daughter. Been a widow for years and always wanted Sam to go and live with her.

He wouldn't consider it. `I'll leave here when I'm carried out and not before', he always said." A tear rolled down Maggie's cheek.

"He may get better," Jess said, hastily.

Maggie shook her head. "His age is against him. I don't think we'll see him back home again."

To Jess's relief Pam arrived and began to fuss over Maggie, so she was able to slip out to Sonata. When she returned to the kitchen Pam told her that she had managed to reassure Mrs Carey that they would be able to take on Sam's duties for the time being, and that Mr Barnes was on his way to give Sonata a `check up'.

To assist Mr Barnes Jess decided to move Sonata to a brighter box near the door. She transferred all the dry straw but it didn't amount to much of a bed. She was between the boxes when the scrunch of car wheels in the yard caught her attention. She went outside and saw a man standing by the open boot of his car, pulling on Wellingtons; he was a tall and well-built, with greying hair and a kind weather-beaten face.

"Sorry I'm late." He shook hands with Jess telling her he was John Barnes. "I know who you are. Adam told us all about you. He's away at his granny's for a few days or he'd have been round here like a shot. He said there was something strange about the stables. It seems the mystery has been solved."

Shyly Jess led the way, saying, "I was just going to move her. She's in the far box which is very dark."

"Right. Let's do that. These old-fashioned stables have their merits but brightness isn't one of them."

Jess untied Sonata and, praying she wouldn't fall over, led her to her new box. Mr Barnes unbuckled the roller and gently removed the rug. Jess took it from him.

"Slow starvation," he said, after a moment of looking at the mare intently. "I dread to think what her teeth are like - if she has any."

He began to examine Sonata, talking to her all the time while he moved slowly from eyes, teeth, heart and hooves to pathetic stringy tail. Then he stood for several minutes looking thoughtful. Jess felt sick with apprehension.

"Teeth like fangs; heart surprisingly strong and feet reasonably short. I expect the old chap trimmed them himself which shows he was well-intentioned."

As he spoke Pam appeared, slipping quietly into the box. Jess relaxed a little but wished grown-ups wouldn't waste time with introductions at such a fraught time!

At last Mr Barnes said, "She'll need a great deal of nursing. I'll run tests to make sure there aren't any hidden problems, such as anaemia, but I think lack of nourishment is the main one. She doesn't seem to be arthritic but we'll find out all we can. Now, I suppose we'd better discuss all this with Mrs Carey."

Upstairs, Mr Barnes chose his words carefully. "Your mare has such long teeth insufficient food has been reaching her stomach."

Mrs Carey did not beat about the bush. Looking him straight in the eye, she said, "She is slowly starving, you mean? What else is wrong?" There was a quaver in her voice.

"She has some sores aggravated by the rug; she's probably riddled with worms but her heart is amazingly strong and so are her lungs."

"What are her feet like?"

"A touch of thrush but hooves not too long. Sam has managed to trim them roughly."

Mrs Carey smiled. "He worked with a blacksmith when he was young. He's done his best - I'm sure of that."

"I'm sure of that too," Mr Barnes said swiftly. "He's done all he could but just as he wouldn't acknowledge his age, I suspect he couldn't accept the mare's age either."

"But how could I let this happen? Seeing her nearly every day and never wondering if she was really well and happy? It's unforgivable!"

Mr Barnes said in a gentle but firm voice, "You've had enough to cope with. You really shouldn't blame yourself."

"What can we do for her? Can we give her a better life?"

Jess stopped breathing. Mr Barnes took so long replying to Mrs Carey that she was forced to start again.

"I'd like to give her a chance and so would Jess. There are practical things to be done such as filing her teeth, worming her, having blood tests and asking the farrier to even up her feet. The sores and the thrush should clear up quite quickly. There is something she will have to find for herself - the will to live - she hasn't much of that at this moment."

Suddenly Pam spoke. "I once helped to restore a pony's will to live. It was Marmalade's dam. She was half frozen in a snowdrift and thought her foal was dead. That was much worse because she was semi-wild with little knowledge of humans. Sonata has been loved and cared for so I'm sure we can restore her confidence."

They were all looking at her and for a second no one spoke. Jess wanted to hug her but kept still, reliving the picture of her parents bringing an exhausted wild pony home, carrying the foal that seemed more dead than alive. Her father had carried Marmalade even though his arms and back were already wracked with pain. Jess, aged six, left to wait at home with her grandmother, had burst into relieved sobs as their blurred, snowy shapes came into view. It was so hard not to do the same now.

Then Mrs Carey said, "Jess dear, so much of this will fall on your shoulders. You have your own pony to look after and school starts very soon. Have I any right to impose more work on you?"

"Oh, but it won't be work, Mrs Carey. It won't seem like work at all!"

"I know my dear, but however it *seems* it will demand some of your time."

She looked enquiringly at Pam.

"Marmalade is hardly any trouble at all; so it isn't as if Jess will be doubling up on stable duties. Her school work will be more demanding next year than this..."

"So it's quite all right!" Jess interrupted her mother triumphantly.

Mrs Carey beamed at her and then asked Mr Barnes to do all he could for Sonata.

He smiled and assured her he would do all he could and now, with Jess perhaps, would sort out what food could be given to her.

Back in the stable Jess listened earnestly to Mr Barnes's instructions.

"Very small, soft feeds of boiled barley, or sugar beet pulp with soft chaff, if she can manage it. Alfafa might be easier for her to eat than ordinary hay and Alfafa nuts soaked and added to other soft food. She'll need four small feeds a day, and an added supplement once a day which I'll bring later. The worry is that she might not want to eat so you can add pulped apple or even honey to get her interested. I'll give you some ointment and dressings and she'll need a modern, lightweight rug that she'll hardly feel on her back. The thrush will clear up quite quickly with the blacksmith's help but it will involve daily dressings."

He pulled out a note pad and wrote down some telephone numbers.

"Try any of these for fodder and straw. They all deliver - even quite small quantities. Now, I must be off to see some cows, but I'll be back this afternoon."

Before he drove away he lowered the window and said, "The children will be back in a few days, so don't be surprised if they turn up."

Watching the car turn into the drive Jess thought he was one of the nicest grown-ups she had met. Suddenly life seemed so much better!

The following days were packed with activity for Jess: scrubbing out feed bins, cleaning the stable windows (having first prised open the covering shutters, not opened for years), and stacking bales of hay and straw after a surly driver had dumped them in the yard. On the Aga barley casseroles bubbled and kettles sang, ready for Sonata's gruel and to melt the ice in Marmalade's trough. A tray was laid on the dresser, all ready with dressings, bandages, ointments and scissors, hospital fashion.

"Maybe I should borrow your uniform," said Jess, drily.

"You certainly may." Pam laughed. "Mrs Carey has decided I needn't wear it, unless I want to."

Maggie re-named the kitchen 'The Ops room'. She entered into the bustle with a will, carrying buckets of hot water, holding bandages, and Sonata's legs while Jess dressed each hoof with great care.

"Better that I'm here than your mum," she told Jess. "Not that I know the first thing about horses, but we don't want Mrs Carey to feel neglected."

Fat chance of that, thought Jess who saw Pam about three times a day.

Mr Barnes visited Sonata again but to Jess's annoyance she was out on Marmalade, taking advantage of the rapid thaw, and missed him.

"Didn't he say anything about Adam?" she demanded. "Is he still away?"

Surprised, Pam shook her head. "No, but he did say Sonata seemed a little brighter."

"Oh good," said Jess off-handedly. Really she was pleased, but for the first time in her life she felt overwhelmed by the presence of grown-ups, and longed for the company of other children.

A local farrier, Mr Cobb, trimmed Sonata's feet and re-set Marmalade's shoes. He told Jess his little daughter had a Shetland pony and belonged to the Pony Club.

"D'you know Adam Barnes?" she asked.

"Oh yes, everyone knows the twins." He straightened up and patted Marmalade. "Nice pony."

A few hours later Pam came out to the stable looking pleased. She said, "A Mrs Bradshaw has just 'phoned inviting you to a Pony Club rally on Friday. She's going to drop a membership form in. Mr Cobb mentioned you this afternoon when he was shoeing her horses. Wasn't that kind of him?"

Jess scowled. "Who is this Mrs Bradshaw?"

"She's the local District Commissioner. She sounded so friendly and said how much she hoped you'd join. She's even lending you a Pony Club manual so you'll have some idea of what happens. Oh - yes, I nearly forgot, she said the Barnes twins are members and would probably be there, and another local boy..."

"Yes, all right, Mum, I know all that. Perhaps I'll join eventually, but I don't know about the rally."

Pam sighed. "Well, if do go it will be very easy. It'll be at a riding school about two miles away."

Chapter 4

It was not so much that Jess hated the idea of going to the rally but more that she dreaded finding herself in the company of the girls who had ridiculed Marmalade. Even if they weren't members (but she was pretty sure they would be), there might be others like them. However, by the end of the week, with all traces of snow having vanished, Jess had no good excuse for not going. She decided that she owed it to Marmalade to give her some fun so set off at a brisk trot, wearing her carefully pressed jacket with a shirt and tie, in place of her thick jersey and anorak. Marmalade was scrupulously clean having been stabled overnight next to Sonata.

In the yard of Berrywood Riding School Jess dismounted and watched as trailers and horseboxes were unloaded of their superior-looking occupants. Most of the ponies were clipped making Marmalade look hairier than ever. Children called greetings to their friends and mothers fussed, giving instructions that were largely ignored.

Nobody took any notice of Jess and she willed Adam to appear, then a tall woman with severely netted grey hair bore down on her, crying, "Ah, there you are. Have you got your membership form?"

Jess produced an envelope from her pocket. The woman opened it, scrutinised the form and cheque then stuffed them into the pocket of her dry, cracked Barbour.

"That's all correct. I'm the Chief Instructor. We'll be riding indoors. Just watch what the others do and follow them in."

She marched off to greet some new arrivals who seemed to be unloading racehorses. A familiar voice caught Jess's attention and, dismayed, she recognised one of Marmalade's adversaries. She appeared from behind a trailer leading a dun pony. A taller girl walked behind her.

"Oh look!" she exclaimed. "It's the Gnu!" and both collapsed with laughter.

Jess ignored them. The first girl attempted to mount but the pony walked around in circles. The taller girl watched and criticized without attempting to help. Only when the pony was viciously jabbed in the mouth did it halt and the girl scrambled into the saddle inelegantly.

After twelve riders and ponies had assembled the Instructor ordered them into the school.

"Mount up! Mount up!" she barked, and in her hurry Jess dropped her whip and had to start again. She was the last to enter the school preceded by a fanfare of whinnying from Marmalade who stood goggle-eyed in the doorway for a second. Scarlet-faced Jess squeezed her on, aware that there was a good deal of giggling among other riders.

The school was large and smart, with great overhead lights, a gallery, and huge mirrors. Catching sight of herself Marmalade stopped abruptly, snorting in amazement. Then she and her reflection whinnied in unison and moved towards one another. The members were now hooting with laughter and, when Jess had to wait while Marmalade touched muzzles with her double, she heard a familiar voice say, "It's a g'nother Gnu!"

Angry now, uncharacteristically she tapped the pony with her whip and, surprised, Marmalade shot forward banging the elegant rump of the next pony.

"Do be careful - you could get kicked," admonished the equally elegant rider, glaring at Jess.

"Sorry," she muttered. Surely the stupid girl must know it wasn't deliberate.

They seemed to spend ages warming up (some needed cooling down, Jess thought). Several younger children were mounted on horses wearing a greater variety of bits and martingales than Jess had ever seen. She supposed these enabled the riders to have some control in absence of any natural ability!

After riding in large circles and changing direction several times the children were asked to line up for a tack inspection. So far, so good, thought Jess, for Marmalade was happy to do what everyone else did in spite of her excitement at this new experience.

A younger boy was ticked off for not having safety stirrups, then the Instructor arrived in front of Marmalade. Jess held her breath and wondered if she should salute. There was a brief inspection of saddle and bridle then a nod of approval and Jess was able to breath again.

"What is this contraption?" The formidable instructor was now in front of the dun pony.

"A dropped noseband, Mrs Trotman."

At least I now know her name, thought Jess, and an apt one!

"Yes, Annette, I recognise it's a dropped noseband but why are you using it?"

"My sister suggested it."

"Oh really! And where is Olivia? Why isn't she here? She is supposed to be helping."

Annette was steeling herself not to look towards the gallery where her sister, Olivia, was trying to shrink.

"She's got a cold, Mrs Trotman."

"That shouldn't stop her riding. Do her good to get out in the air."

"She was afraid she'd give it to the ponies."

The members shrieked with laughter. Even Mrs Trotman's mouth twitched. She made Annette dismount and adjust the noseband.

"That pony's behind the bit. It doesn't need a dropped noseband, just

31

positive riding. If anyone else is tempted to use one please make sure your pony can breathe."

At least Annette was giggling with the rest of them, Jess observed. After lecturing them on the uses and abuses of gadgets, Mrs Trotman said they could ride over trotting poles to prepare for jumping. Jess brightened up. She and Marmalade loved jumping.

"Now one at a time, remembering distance equals safety. Walk the first round, then trot."

Jess watched several riders go round then it was her turn.

"Nice, sturdy pony," said Mrs Trotman. "Should be able to jump."

"Oh, she's brilliant," said Jess, blushing.

Sure that Marmalade would happily follow the others, Jess was shocked when she snaked up to the line of poles, snorting suspiciously, then stopped.

Mrs Trotman's cry, "Keep her straight" changed to "Push her on."

Jess squeezed until she thought her legs would drop off and, at last, Marmalade put a hoof over the first pole as cautiously as a swimmer testing the water. The other hooves followed and Marmalade kept going over the five other poles but with exaggerated caution.

"Come round again. If you think she's going to stop use your whip."

Jess hated hitting her pony but as they approached the poles again she lightly tapped her while squeezing like mad. Marmalade went over the poles without faltering.

Next, they had to trot over the poles. Jess was allowed to follow a schoolmaster pony and had no problems but, when the poles were followed by a tiny jump, Marmalade again stopped. Jess tapped her and she flew up into the air like a stag, landing with Jess halfway up her neck and painfully banging her nose. Eyes smarting, she made for the end of the line but was told to go round again. More by luck than judgement she went round quite smoothly and earned a, "Well done."

No one else stopped but Annette hit her pony so much it made Jess wince and drew a sharp reprimand from Mrs Trotman. From the gallery her older sister hissed advice which was clearly confusing her. Jess felt some sympathy for her although she had been so rude about Marmalade. Her pony was sluggish and seemed to dislike jumping, but what had caused him to hollow his back and stick his head in the air?

All too soon the children were told they could now jump a small course. It was a nice course, with no tight turns and nothing higher than two feet, but the jumps were all coloured, miniature show jumps, unfamiliar to Marmalade. Very determinedly Jess rode towards the first fence, a blue and white plank with a rail above it. Marmalade's ears were pricked and she went smoothly from trot into canter but, at the last moment, she dug her hooves in and Jess shot up her neck and nearly fell off. She righted herself quickly and turned Marmalade round to try again.

"Hold on," called Mrs Trotman, and removed the rail. The jump was now really tiny, but again Marmalade stopped.

"This time really whack her."

Jess tapped her: Marmalade hesitated but at last she jumped. Several children called, "Well done," but others grumbled among themselves that Jess was holding them up.

"Don't try another one, just go round and over that one again, then finish."

Marmalade went over more smoothly and confidently and, with great relief, Jess rode her to the end of the line.

"What's wrong with that pony?" demanded Mrs Trotman and someone, in a loud whisper replied, "Oh, she's brilliant."

Jess said she thought she didn't like coloured jumps and that she never refused at home.

"Where's home?"

"Exmoor. We jump streams and low walls and banks."

"I see. Well, your pony will have to be taught to jump what *you* want it to jump; you must practice hard at home. Now, we really must get on."

There were a few discreet cheers. Jess was not asked to jump again. She watched the others progress to slightly higher jumps. Two people struck her as very good; a girl on a beautiful chestnut mare that seemed to flow rather than just move, and a boy on a sweet cob that was not very stylish but looked as if it were smiling. The boy looked vaguely familiar.

At last the rally ended. The children all lined up to say, "Thank you, Mrs Trotman," in chorus.

Jess lost no time in leaving, sending Marmalade into a brisk trot along the drive.

"Hang on," came a shout and she turned to see the boy on the cob catching up; then she realised he was the tractor driver who had directed her to the bridlepath on her first ride. She felt embarrassed that she hadn't recognised him but when she tried to apologise he laughed and said, "It's the hat, it makes me look quite different."

"I like your horse," Jess said.

"He's Mum's, she bred him from a Welsh mare and a hunter. I ride him more than she does in the holidays." He patted the horse affectionately. "Old Trotters was a bit hard on you," he commented. "She's never very nice to new members. Really she likes to work with the team members."

"Are you in a team?"

"Yes, but only just. Don't worry about old Trotters; the rallies are usually taken by Sally Newman. She owns Berrywood but she's away. I expect you'll have her next time."

Only there won't be a next time thought Jess with a determined set of her chin.

Chapter 5

Although it was the last day of the holidays Jess was in good spirits as she unblocked the yard drain, and listened to the birds whose voices were swelling with enjoyment at the sudden burst of sunshine. Then she heard a curious swishing and trundling sound, a bit like a wheelbarrow travelling at high speed. Puzzled, she walked across the yard and narrowly missed being hit by a skateboard. It bore a rosy-faced girl who gasped an apology, halted abruptly, then jumped about eighteen inches off the ground, the board miraculously going with her.

"Hi - I'm Susan Barnes. Adam's coming but he stopped to talk to your pony. I wanted to meet you today and not wait 'til ghastly school!"

Completely disarmed, Jess threw her gloves on top of the bucket of muddy straw and said, "Hello, I'm Jess. I've been unblocking the drain."

Before Susan could speak her twin arrived also on a skateboard, pursued by a yapping wire-haired dachshund.

"This is Marmite," said Adam as the exuberant little dog put muddy paws on Jess's knees and barked a greeting. "He's seriously self-important. Mum says it's because he's the smallest member of the family and terrified of being overlooked."

Jess laughed and said that was easily done as he was so close to the ground.

"May we please see the old mare?" Susan asked, eagerly. "Dad says you're doing brilliantly with her."

Jess flushed with pleasure and led the way into the stable where, to her delight, Sonata glanced around to see her visitors and whickered a gentle greeting.

"Oh, she's sweet," Susan said, going into the box without hesitation and stroking her handsome nose. "Dad was afraid she'd given up."

"She still looks like a toast rack, "said Jess," but she seems happier. This morning she whickered at me and nudged me. I gave her a sugar lump that she sucked for ages. Better not tell your dad – he'd probably worry about her teeth."

The twins laughed and Adam said that at her age it probably didn't matter. "Sometimes," he admitted, "I give Pie a lump of sugar, just as a treat."

Jess grinned, remembering his visit and the empty sugar bowl. She suggested taking Sonata for a walk in the paddock; so they all trooped out with Marmite dancing around them. Marmalade hurried over, encrusted with mud having rolled over and over after her ride. Marmite barked very close to her nose and she charged him, head down bull-like, but he skipped smartly out of the way and began to circle her, yapping. She shook her head and trotted at him. They played in this way for several minutes then the children grew tired of Marmite's voice and told him to shut up. He gave one more defiant yap, looking straight at them.

Susan giggled, "He is dreadful. He can't bear to lose face. Our other dog, Siani, is completely different, gentle and thoughtful. A typical labrador, I s'pose."

"I've never met a dachshund properly before," said Jess. "I think he's really funny and cute."

"Hmm," said Adam, "so does he."

They took Sonata back to her stable and helped Jess scrub out her hooves, dry them thoroughly, then pack them with cotton wool covered with Stockholm tar. As each foot was finished she covered it with a very thick, large sock, which she fastened around the cannon bone with a stable bandage over gamgee.

"That's a brilliant method," enthused Susan.

"Mum's idea," Jess said. "She used to work with horses. The socks last quite a while because she isn't shod and stands on such thick straw."

"Has Dad seen it?"

"Yes, he approved."

"What happened to the old man? Did he die?" Adam asked suddenly.

"No," said Jess, "he's improving. His daughter's staying in his cottage and visits him every day. He can talk a little now, but he can't walk. The nurses think he's a wonder."

Leaving Sonata comfortable and contented, they went indoors to meet Pam. She had seen them from an upstairs window and had a pot of tea and warm lardy cake waiting for them. They sat around the kitchen table chattering like magpies, swapping information about school, the village, Exmoor and their best friends. Jess felt as relaxed as if she'd known the twins for years.

She studied their faces while they were occupied eating. Although they were alike, having the same thick fair hair and grey eyes, Susan's face was broader, with high cheekbones and a determined-looking chin. Adam's face was rounder and had a gentler look.

The telephone rang. At a nod from Pam, who had been summoned by Mrs Carey's bell, Jess answered it and found the caller was the twins' mother. She suggested Jess might like to go home with her children for lunch. Jess accepted without hesitation.

"You can meet Tara and have your first skateboard lesson," Susan said. "Did you go to the rally? We were still at Granny's or we'd have been there."

"Yes, I didn't enjoy it much."

The twins exchanged knowing grins.

"Old Trotters," they said, in unison.

"It was partly her," Jess admitted. "She was really unfriendly, but the children were just as bad."

"Ali can't have been there. She'd have made friends with you," Susan said. "She's one of our best friends. You'll meet her tomorrow at school. Her name is really Alison, of course."

"She hasn't got a pony of her own," Adam told Jess. "She borrows a Berrywood one, a grey gelding called Linus and would love to own him..."

Susan interrupted him. "Her dad keeps sending her airline tickets to go out to Paraguay and she sends them back, asking him to send money instead, so she can buy Linus."

"Why doesn't she live with her parents?" Jess asked, puzzled.

"She lives with her mum and granny, only her mum is in London during the week. Their cottage is about half a mile from us. Her parents are divorced and, sometimes, Ali feels very angry with her dad. Tell us more about the rally - who else did you meet?"

Jess launched into a detailed description and, when she reached the bit about the sisters, Adam broke in with, "Oh, the Wadham-Smiths!" then added dismissively, "They can't ride for nuts, specially the older one."

"Only she mustn't be corrected," said Susan. Then in an affected voice, "My deah, she is such a genius and so delicately balanced she must nevah, nevah be upset."

The twins giggled and Susan went on, "She's their mother's pet and terribly spoilt. The mother is awful, always bragging and putting other people down. She never says anything nice about other children."

"It's not surprising they're so awful, then," Jess commented.

"I think the younger one would be all right on her own," said Adam. "The trouble is she's always being told she's wonderful but not quite as wonderful as her sister; so she's bound to be a bit rotted up."

"I only met one nice person," Jess said. "The boy from the farm on a lovely cob."

"Oh, Tom Latcham. He's cool," said Susan.

When Jess had finished her account she said with determination, "I never want to see any of them ever again."

The twins looked dismayed and protested, saying that she'd miss lots of fun and, anyway, rallies with Sally Newman were quite different.

"But the members are the same," Jess said.

"You only met a few of them," Adam said, reasonably. "Honestly, they're not all horrible, and we don't just have rallies; we have a show, a one-day event and a hunter trial."

"And camp," added Susan.

"Our ponies have improved by going to rallies," Adam went on, "especially Tara who needed to work with lots of different ponies. Isn't that right, sis?"

Susan nodded but frowned at him.

Jess would not be swayed by their arguments. She changed the subject by pointing out it was nearly one o'clock and wouldn't they be late for lunch?

Laburnum Lodge was a prettier and much smaller than The Elms. Comfortably furnished with plenty of squashy sofas and armchairs and yards of crammed bookshelves, there was evidence that pets as well as people lived there. There were two dog baskets and a cat igloo in the living room and rugs thrown over favourite chairs.

Adam had a hamster called George. He lived in an adapted square playpen in a corner of Adam's bedroom; a huge adventure playground filled with cubes and tunnels, wheels and climbing frames. George was fast asleep inside a little wooden hut but Jess had a glimpse of his iridescent fur, the colour of sunset.

Susan had an aquarium in the sitting-room. She knew all the fish by name and swore they distinguished her face from Adam's.

Visiting the ponies was top priority after lunch but Jess wondered if she would be able to stagger to the paddock. Mrs Barnes, who insisted Jess should call her Lin, as all the twins' friends did, believed that to do justice to her cooking one had to have second and even third helpings. Jess marvelled that the twins were not fat but, like her, were small and light for their eleven years.

Their ponies were in a paddock near to the house and came to the fence when they heard the twins' voices. Despite her winter coat and untidy mane, Tara's quality was obvious.

"She's lovely," Jess enthused, "and I like her name."

"It's short for Tarantula," said Adam, grinning.

"Tarantella, you twit," said Susan. "He's just jealous 'cause she beat Pie in the under fourteen jumping at the Pony Club show last year."

Adam sat on the top bar of the gate and, putting his arms around Pie's neck, gave him a smacking kiss on his pink nose.

"He's really daft with that pony," said Susan.

"Did you have ponies before these?" Jess asked.

"Not of our own. We had two tiny ponies on loan from the same owner. When we outgrew them they just went back home. We'd be hopeless at selling ponies on."

"So should I," said Jess. "We'll never sell Marmalade, she's family. When she was first rescued she and her dam lived in the old scullery next to the boiler, like in the olden days when people and animals lived under the same roof."

"Gosh, your mum is nice for a nurse," said Susan, then looked horrified at what she'd said. "I mean it's nice she's not fussy the way some nurses are."

Jess grinned. "It's all right. I know what you mean. We know lots of nurses who think children and animals should be kept apart 'cause animals are covered with germs. Mum's not a bit like that."

"Why don't people consider that animals are at risk from us?" Adam said.

At that moment a huge black cat appeared and started to weave around Jess's legs purring like a mowing machine. Jess bent down to stroke it.

"That's Magic, Dad's cat," Susan told her. "He says she's our only civilised pet. He's always complaining about the dogs' behaviour and saying if we behaved like that he'd have put us down."

Jess laughed and said she thought their labrador, Siani, was civilised.

"She is until bedtime," said Adam, "then she whines outside the bedroom door until Mum lets her in, and she insists on sleeping across the bottom of their bed."

They gave the ponies a final pat and went to collect skateboards and give Jess her first lesson.

Thanks to Susan and Adam, Jess was far less worried about going to a new school than she 'd expected to be. They caught the school bus together, and even the twins admitted to knowing only half the passengers. Other buses arrived with theirs, spilling children out in their hordes, or so it seemed to Jess, whose confidence was now ebbing. With quick understanding Susan said, "Come on, we'll go to the office and find out which class you're in. There are only four classes in our year and we're not in the same one; so you've a fifty-fifty chance of being with one of us."

Jess found she was in Adam's class and wondered if he would still be nice when he was with his mates. He was exactly the same to her as he had been at home and she was readily accepted as his friend.

The work that morning was not too taxing; in fact, Jess gradually realised she was slightly ahead, perhaps because she'd been to a much smaller school. Quite relaxed by break-time she tore off with Adam to find Susan and meet Alison.

Half way across the playground she recognised Alison from the twins' description - `tall and slim with short, dark, auburn curls and looking a bit like a wild colt'.

"Although Ali lives quite near us she has to go on a different bus as ours gets full." Adam felt it was necessary to explain.

"I'm in Susan's class so I only have to put up with one of them."
Alison laughed. She had sparkling sapphire blue eyes and a most engaging smile.

"Only she's at the top end," said Susan, grinning. "We've been in trouble already and made to sit apart. I was telling Ali about Sonata, and you rescuing her. She's dying to see her."

"And Marmalade," put in Adam. "You'll love her."

"But not according to the ghastly Wadham-Smith's," Alison suggested. "Susan told me about that awful rally. Tell you what, let's all go for a ride together next weekend. I'll ask Sally if I can borrow Linus. I can't wait to get on a pony again. It was quite fun in London. I even got into the Chamber of Horrors without being asked my age, but I've missed you and the horses – the only ones I saw were police horses."

With their plans having been made, the rest of the week flew by. Jess was slightly annoyed when her mother refused to let her see her friends after school and insisted that, for the first week, she must concentrate on sorting out how much time she was going to need for homework and how to fit stable duties in before and after school.

"With the evenings lighter you'll have bags of time to ride," Pam said, reasonably, "but this week you should sort out your timetable."

On Saturday morning the twins and Alison rode down the drive on the dot of ten o'clock. Half-an-hour passed while Alison met Sonata, and Maggie brought out lemonade for everyone.

At last Sonata was left with a small succulent feed which she nuzzled experimentally before taking one or two mouthfuls. She listened for a minute to the departing hoof-beats but did not answer Marmalade's farewell whinny.

Alison was riding the fourteen-two Linus she talked so much about. He was a rather spindly-looking pony with a slightly ewe neck. Jess was not much taken with him but, as Alison so clearly was, she didn't say anything. He certainly walked out well, taking up a position beside Tara, while Pie and Marmalade matched their paces in the rear. They rode for a mile, going past the lane to Tom Latcham's farm and on for several hundred yards then turned left into a woodland drive which, after a few yards, was barred by a field gate with a hunting gate alongside.

"This is our cross-country training area," Adam explained. "The owner lets Pony and Riding Clubs use it."

"You mean the late owner," said Susan. "Lord Connor died at Christmas and his heir is a very distant cousin. No one knows anything about him except he's a business man, but there's a rumour he doesn't want riders on the estate and, as these aren't official bridle-paths, he could stop us."

"It's more than a rumour," Adam said. "Mrs Bradshaw has talked about it to Ali's mum who's a barrister. She thinks by such regular use over many years a right of way might have been established, but his agent has asked for a list of regular users so he can assess wear-and-tear and damage. It sounds as if he won't be friendly."

He glanced at Alison for her comments but she was trying to open the hunting gate. Every time she positioned the pony alongside and leaned down to grab the lever he moved away.

"If we go ahead he's bound to follow," Susan suggested.

"It won't teach him anything," said Alison.

"Yes it will, if we shut the gate after us. That way he'll have to stand or stay on the other side."

Susan's idea worked and they took up their old positions, calmly walking through the sun-dappled wood that would soon be a carpet of bluebells.

Jess beamed happily. "How big is the wood, Adam?"

He considered for a moment. "A few hundred acres. There's a pheasant-rearing area we can't enter but it's only a small part. The jumps start soon. Perhaps we'd better go in single file." Politely he held Pie back so Jess could go ahead.

Susan, in the lead, called, "We're going to trot."

Jess felt a tingle of excitement. Natural-looking jumps should hold no fear for Marmalade.

Adam called in his thoughtful way, "Each fence has a lower option and there's nothing too terrible."

After jumping several nice logs they reached the first course fence, low fixed poles that all the ponies flew. Then they jumped a brush fence, all taking the lower option, and on to a series of rustic fences which bothered no one.

"This is such fun," Jess called over her shoulder and Adam beamed in agreement.

"Are you happy with a palisade?" he called.

"Don't know. We've never met one."

"Well, here it comes."

Marmalade flew the unfamiliar fence while Alison rode wide of it, not wanting to over-face Linus, who was an unknown quantity as a jumper.

When they stopped for a breather, Jess asked, "What's Linus's history?"

"Don't know but I expect he's a good pony who's been spoilt. Sally hasn't had him long." Alison patted the thin neck fondly. "I'm really pleased with him. He's jumped everything I've asked him to, but I'm not going to ask too much of him today. Isn't Marmalade an ace jumper!'

Jess could have hugged her. "I wish old Trotters could see her today. Who cares about stupid show jumps?"

"Shall we go to the stream?" asked Susan. "We can wade through, or jump where it's lined with sleepers."

They agreed eagerly. Marmalade had a little stream running through one of her Exmoor paddocks and often jumped it for fun; so she had no problem with this one. Alison decided to wade across but Susan and Tara had to splash in ahead of her to give Linus confidence, then they returned to jump a narrower part.

They had all changed positions and Adam was now in the lead. Suddenly a deer shot across the track startling Pie so that he stopped abruptly and sat down. Slowly, Adam slid off backwards and somehow managed to bang his nose. Pie stood stock still looking embarrassed.

"How could you possibly bang your nose from that position?" asked Susan, totally unsympathetic, although a trickle of blood was running down Adam's lips.

Everyone dismounted and Jess held all the reins while Susan became elder-sisterly and told Adam to lie flat. He did so.

"Ugh, it's disgusting. I'b swallowing by blood."

"We should put something cold down his back," said Alison. "What could we use? A stirrup?"

Adam shot upright, blood spattering his front.

"I'b not habing anything shoved down by back."

"Lie down, you twit," said Susan. "Do you hurt anywhere?"

"No, but I'b lost lots of blood."

"Not really," said Alison. "Certainly not a pint, which is what donors give."

"Oh good," Adam said, with a hint of sarcasm.

"Hasn't anyone got a mobile phone?" asked Jess. "I'm sorry but I didn't think to bring mine – you see, it never works on Exmoor."

"And there's no signal here – ever," said Susan. "Mum says we must never ride alone here, especially jumping."

The ponies shoved Jess impatiently then tried to graze. Alison took Linus from her and Susan loosened all the girths to give them a breather.

Adam began to feel chilled and uncomfortable lying on the ground. He removed his hat.

"I'b okay now."

"Shouldn't rush," Susan advised. "P'raps we'd better go back to the stream and clean you up."

Adam sat up cautiously, then slowly got to his feet. He touched his nose gingerly then said in his normal voice, "Seems all right. I've got a disgusting taste in my mouth but, at last, I can speak properly."

"You don't feel faint, do you?" enquired Alison but was rewarded with a withering look.

At the stream they rummaged in their pockets for tissues or handkerchiefs. Susan produced a rag smelling of Silvo, Adam an apple core (which he slipped to Pie when the other ponies were not looking), and Alison a ball of grubby tissues. Only Jess had a large handkerchief that she was pretty sure she hadn't blown into. Adam shuddered but allowed Susan to clean him up after wetting the hanky in the stream.

"Ouch, it's icy!" he exclaimed.

Susan worked on relentlessly, holding his chin in a vice-like grip and trying not to giggle at his look of frozen agony.

"There, you look a lot better now. I'll give this to Mum to boil, Jess."

"Oh, don't bother, Susan."

"No, Mum will insist. It can go in with the operation sheets and be sterilised."

Jess was not sure that she wanted her handkerchief that badly.

Adam remounted carefully and, without further mishaps they rode home slowly, leaving Jess at her drive. Marmalade walked crab-wise, looking back whinnying loud goodbyes to her new friends. Jess put her in the stable next to Sonata and gave them both a small feed. Marmalade's was a handful each of chaff and coarse mix, while Sonata had a small amount of sugar beet pulp.

Discussing Adam's accident with her mother she wondered how they would have coped if he'd broken something. Pam removed soaking stirrup irons and the snaffle bit from the washing-up bowl and rather pointedly, scoured it with Vim.

"I hope one of you would have ridden for help and the rest would have made Adam as warm and comfortable as possible. It just shows how you should ride in company, especially where a mobile phone doesn't work."

"Oh Mum! If that had been a rule I'd never have ridden at home."

"Yes, I suppose you're right," Pam conceded, "but the moor is more open and everyone knew you. Certainly you shouldn't ride over jumping courses alone."

"Adam's fall had nothing to do with jumping; I said it was caused by a deer." Jess was beginning to feel irritated.

"Right, and of course lots of accidents are unavoidable, but I don't want you to ride over that jumping course alone."

"Don't worry, it's likely to be out-of-bounds soon," Jess said, grumpily, and began to dry her stirrups.

"Not with a tea towel," said Pam, sighing. "Now do please make a space for the lunch things."

Adam suffered no ill-effects. By five o'clock he was reluctantly playing Monopoly with Susan, Jess and Alison while waiting for tea to be ready.

"Board games should be spelt B O R E D," he complained, yawning exaggeratedly.

"No-one forced you to play," snapped Susan. "Do wake up. You have to go to the Community Chest."

The twins' mother put her head round the door. "Sorry to interrupt but Mrs Bradshaw wants to talk to you Jess. She tried The Elms first. Something to do with the next rally."

"I'm not going to the next rally, or any rally," said Jess crossly. "What does she want me for?"

Lin smiled sympathetically. "Come to the 'phone and find out. She's really very nice".

Adam snorted, and Alison said she'd play Jess's turn.

"Bet she wants Marmalade as the summer raffle prize," said Adam, grinning.

"Hullo, hullo - oh, there you are," boomed Mrs Bradshaw. "Jess dear, I've a great favour to ask you. We want to borrow a native pony for a stable rally and wonder if we may have Marmalade. She's probably the only Exmoor for miles around, so will make it most interesting. There'll be a lecture with slides on all the pony breeds, then our speaker wants to particularly discuss the characteristics of our live model. We're so lucky to have booked an eminent judge and breeder; so we expect everyone to attend. It will be a three-line-whip."

She laughed uproariously for several seconds, then suddenly barked, "Are you there, Jess?"

"Oh – er - yes, Mrs Bradshaw."

"Are there any problems? The rally will be at Berrywood so very handy for you. Do say we may have her."

All the while Mrs Bradshaw had been talking, Jess had been frantically scrabbling in her mind for an excuse; failing, she heard her voice as if it were someone else's, saying, "Yes - yes, of course."

"Excellent," enthused Mrs Bradshaw. "You'll read all about it in the forthcoming newsletter, and I shall contact you personally nearer the rally. Thank you so much, Jess. Most grateful. Goodbye."

Jess flopped back into her chair with a face like thunder.

"Oh no! She's agreed to give Marmalade as the raffle prize," said Adam, grinning.

"You're almost right," Jess said.

"Was she awful?" demanded Susan.

Jess sighed heavily. "No, she was quite nice really. She wants Marmalade to be the model for a talk on native ponies at half-term."

"Oh gosh!" Susan understood at once. "And you couldn't refuse."

"No, she sort of bulldozed me, not giving me time to think."

"Grown-ups are jolly good at that," commented Adam. "'Specially teachers. I got roped in to help with some silly..."

"Shut up, Adam," cried Susan. "We want to hear from Jess. Where will the rally be?"

"At Berrywood Stables. A famous judge is coming and there'll be slides."

"Boring! No one will turn up."

"We have to, Adam. She said it was a three-line-whip then nearly died laughing."

"Pity she didn't."

"Why should I lend my pony for a bunch of beastly, stuck-up brats to poke fun at and say foul things?"

"They won't be able to with grown-ups there," Alison suggested. "Anyway, we'll all give support. Really it's quite flattering to you and Marmalade. She must approve of you both or she wouldn't have asked you, and 'specially with a famous judge coming."

Jess refused to be swayed. "There probably isn't another pure bred native pony in the whole of Surrey. I s'pect she didn't have any choice."

"Well, all the more reason to be proud of your native pony if they're so rare in these parts."

"Alison, I am proud of her; it's other people who despise her."

"Then give them the chance to find out how ignorant and stupid they are."

They were called to tea, sumptuous and laid on the large kitchen table. Muffins running with butter, homemade biscuits and fruitcake, a great variety of sandwiches and anchovy toast, could hardly fail to raise anyone's spirits, but still Jess looked mutinous.

"You can't back out now you've promised," Alison pointed out reasonably. "Try to see it as a challenge."

"Yes, we'll all work on her coat and make her look wonderful. We'll wash her mane and tail and separate every hair, and we'll scrub and polish her hooves as if she's going to a show."

The others were caught up in Susan's enthusiasm and slowly Jess cheered up.

"And don't worry," said Adam, then, with uncharacteristic belligerence, added, "If anyone is rude about Marmalade I'll duff them up."

Chapter 6

The children spent some of their break-time working out a schooling and fitness programme for the ponies. They would have short rides on their two easier homework evenings and two long rides at weekends.

It surprised Jess when, a week later, Adam tore into the yard on his bike only an hour after they had left the school bus and, particularly, as Monday meant maths and French homework and no riding. His face was flushed and he looked worried.

Jess had just finished tidying the yard and was about to put the broom away.

"What's up, Adam?" She grabbed the handlebars as the bike veered towards the ground after a perilously abrupt and screeching stop.

Breathlessly, Adam said, "Where can we talk without being overheard?"

She stared at him then swiftly led the way into the stable.

"What's the matter? You're in a state."

Now Adam drew in a long breath. "I was in the hall cupboard checking my cricket gear when the 'phone rang. Dad was just going out so he picked it up in the hall and I heard him talking to Mrs Carey. I s'pose I should have walked out but conversations are always being overheard in our house with people ringing at all hours; so I just went on rummaging but - well - listening..."

"Yes - yes, do go on, Adam."

He took another gulp of air and continued, "I only heard Dad's side, of course, but it was clear Mrs Carey was asking about Sonata 'cause Dad said she must be feeling a bit better because the sores and thrush were clearing up, but he was seriously worried about her lack of appetite. He praised you a lot and said no one could give Sonata better care and that was the worry; if he, you and Pam can't make her better – well - she just might not be meant to get better." He ended in a rush.

Jess felt a lump in her throat and tears were very close but she didn't care; Adam never called girls wimps the way some of the boys did at school.

He looked at her in distress and gave her shoulder a clumsy pat. "I thought you had to know," he said, miserably.

"What d'you mean? Know what? They're not going to put her down?"

"No," said Adam hastily. "Honestly - not yet and I know Dad would tell you but he said he wasn't sure how much longer..."

He stopped. Tears were pouring down Jess's cheeks. He pulled a filthy handkerchief out of his jeans pocket and gave it to her.

"Please don't cry, Jess. I'm sure we can do something, that's why I came round straight away. I didn't even wait to tell Susan. I've had this idea. You've heard about cows giving their milk more easily if they're listening to music, and racehorses travelling better - and even plants growing faster?"

Jess nodded, mopping her eyes.

"Well, let's try playing music to Sonata. Let's play tapes, DC's and the radio - anything we can lay our hands on, so there's music nearly all the time. We must try."

Jess gulped and nodded. "Sh - shall we tell the grown-ups?"

"No," said Adam swiftly. "At least only your mum. She'll have to know as we'll need someone to keep the music going while you're at school. I shan't say anything to Dad. I'm not sure why 'cause I don't feel badly about overhearing him, but grown-ups can get silly idea - they might think we're too involved and not working at school."

"Yes, I think you're right and Mum will have to know but she's brilliant at keeping secrets. When shall we start?"

Without hesitation, Adam replied, "Now, as soon as I've got some gear together. Dad's out, of course, and Mum's visiting our neighbour. With a bit of luck she won't be back."

"I've got a transistor and a cassette player," said Jess.

"Right, we'll pool what we've got. We'll need a long lead and adaptor. What about tapes and CD's?"

"I've only five," Jess said, "and they're all pop or jazz."

"Well, I doubt if she's developed a taste for any particular music unless she's heard a lot. We'll have to experiment and try to find out what she likes."

Adam sounded so enthusiastic that Jess had to restrain herself from hugging him which she was sure he wouldn't appreciate. He grabbed his bike saying, "I'll get off now and be back as soon as possible."

Jess let herself into Sonata's box and put her arms around the mare's slender neck. "You must try hard to get better - we all want you to so much - all of us, including Marmalade. Don't you want to get better? Oh, I wish you could talk. We'll look after you so well and give you a really happy life, I promise."

Sonata twitched her ears and dropped her soft muzzle onto Jess's arm. She gave a long deep sigh and did not move away although her mane became damp with Jess's tears.

Struggling to be brave, Jess wiped her eyes with Adam's hanky. She thought of her father whose mind and will refused to accept the disease that tortured his body for so long. He hadn't wanted to die in spite of his pain. It was so unfair that the chance to go on fighting had been taken from him when, very suddenly, his heart had failed. It hurt Jess so much to think of Sonata dying but was it equally unfair to try to keep her going if, really, she just wanted to stop? But what did she want? How could they know? Suddenly she felt a desperate need to talk to her mother.

In the kitchen Pam put down a tray with a clatter and gasped. "Jess - your face - what have you done? Have you been in a fight?"

Jess grinned. "I expect it's dirt from Adam's hanky." She opened her hand and revealed the filthy rag. "Better go in the washing machine."

"Better not," replied Pam. "I'll get him a new one. Has he been cleaning his bike with it?"

"Probably. Anyway, I think it's one of mine so it doesn't matter. Mum, I've got something important to talk about."

And she launched into her story becoming more confident while Pam listened without interrupting.

When Jess had finished she said, "I agree with Adam's scheme. I don't think his father would keep Sonata going if he thought there was no more hope. I'm sure we should try. Music is therapeutic although we don't know quite how or why. Tell me what I can do to help. You've only got your little radio and old cassette player..."

"Oh, it's all right, Mum, Adam's bringing loads of gear. We'll need your help with keeping the music going while I'm at school."

"Well, I can certainly do that. Now do go and wash your face, Jess. You look scary!"

Less than half-an-hour later Adam and Susan arrived with their bike carriers full of electrical gadgets, CD's and tapes. Susan was caught up in Adams' enthusiasm. "Should we keep the music going all night?"

Adam and Jess considered this but decided it might be overdoing things and Pam might not agree anyway.

"Just suppose she hates music," Jess said, with sudden doubt.

"Oh, she won't," Adam said, confidently. "All horses love music."

They set to work carrying equipment into the stable. Adam sorted out leads and adaptors.

"I can't see a power point," he said, looking around. "We could use the light socket at a pinch but it's not considered really safe."

Jess remembered noticing a power point in the hay store adjoining the stable. It had once been a wash house. The children went to investigate and found the point in the party wall under a tiny cobweb-covered window.

"We can run a lead through to the stable providing the window opens," said Adam.

"It doesn't," said Jess. "I don't think it's meant to."

"Bother, we might have to break it."

"Adam, we can't," Jess said. "It's not our property."

He gave her a look of exasperation. "It's a matter of life and death, Jess. Do we ask permission and let Mrs Carey know what we're doing?"

"Hang on," said Susan. "The frame looks rotten. I think we could ease the glass out, or maybe the whole window."

"Right, I'll use my knife," said Adam. He always carried a combined penknife and hoofpick.

He carefully inserted the knife between the wooden frame and the wall. It gave at once, crumbling a little as the wood was so rotten. It took him a few minutes of careful probing before he could lift the window out.

"Oh, well done," said Jess. "We can easily put it back again later."

It only took minutes to set up a system that would provide hours of music. That was the easy bit; sorting out the programme was another matter.

"Not Heavy Metal, Susan," Adam said. "I don't think she's the type, not yet anyway."

"That's really snobby, Adam, just 'cause she's a thoroughbred. I s'pose you think Pie would only like pop or rap."

"Now who's being snobby? You're just showing how ignorant you are. I don't think classical music is posh, it's just that it might be quiet and gentle for her to start with."

"Oh, what about some Wagner then?" said Susan with acid sarcasm.

"Shut up you two," intervened Jess, who was fast learning that the twins' arguments could go on and on, becoming increasingly silly. She picked up a tape and examined the label.

"Themes from Films; this should be fine."

Adam groaned. "One of Granny's favourites."

Susan opened her mouth but her words were drowned by the music for 'Lawrence of Arabia'.

Adam swiftly reduced the volume and, drily, said, "Let's hope she doesn't decide she's a camel."

Even Susan laughed, then for several minutes the children silently watched Sonata for any response. She had not touched the net of soaked hay tied up in the corner, but had taken a few mouthfuls of a feed topped with pulped apples and honey.

Quiet footsteps caught their attention and Pam slipped inside with a mug in one hand and a tea towel over her arm.

"I heard the tape start but it's fine now," she said, then, shushed by Jess, stood silently beside them. Every now and then Sonata's ears twitched but the children could see no sign that she was listening.

"What do you think, Mum?" Jess whispered.

"Much too soon," said Pam, "but I think she's quite relaxed. Can you two stay for supper?"

"Thanks but Mum's expecting us back," replied Susan and looked at her watch. "We'd better go."

Jess picked up the spare equipment and helped Adam to pack it into his bike carrier.

"Let it run for the full four hours," he advised.

"She'll be in bed," Pam said. "Anyway, I'll turn it off before I go to bed."

"Great, Mum," said Jess. She walked along the drive beside the twins, thanking them profusely for their help.

Slightly embarrassed, Adam said, "No hass - really. Just hope it works."

In the kitchen Jess ate her supper without noticing it. "It will work, won't it?" she asked Pam more than once.

Patiently her mother said they could only try and that Sonata seemed to have reached a 'plateau'. She'd visibly improved but now things were bound to go more slowly as there was so much building-up to be done. She offered Jess a second helping but she shook her head.

"No thanks, Mum. You will warn me if Mrs Carey - if she decides...."

"Jess, I wouldn't dream of not talking to you, nor would John Barnes. He's coming to see her next week - just for a routine check-up so don't look so worried."

Mucking out had been a slow procedure with plenty of leaning on pitchfork handle while minutely studying Sonata for any overnight improvement. Jess had to run to catch the school bus. She struggled to regain her breath and to disentangle her bag and coat so the door could close, while the twins bombarded her with questions. At length she was able to say, "I couldn't see that she was any different."

"But no worse?" persisted Susan.

"No and quite happy. I left her listening to Brahms."

Susan grinned. "Poor mare!"

"Oh shut up, Susan," said Adam with unusual asperity. "Jess, you know Dad was going on a call when Mrs Carey rang last evening?"

Jess nodded.

"It's so awful - it was a friend of his, a vet - about three miles away..."

Impatiently, Susan interrupted: "A mare and foal had been attacked and Dad's friend wanted a second opinion."

Jess stared at her. "Attacked! How?"

"Knifed," said Susan. "Deliberately knifed. I'd like to get hold of the vicious beast..." Her voice went out of control and her eyes filled with tears.

"The mare was killed." Adam took up the awful story. His distress was equal to Susan's but anger seemed to give him an added strength. "The foal was cut about the head but alive, probably because it panicked and struggled. The owner heard it's frantic whinnying and rushed out but didn't see anyone. Dad said the mare would have died instantly as the knife went straight into the brain, like a captive bolt pistol. He said only an expert could have done it."

In a nearly normal voice Susan added, "A butcher perhaps, or slaughterer or - even a vet."

"The foal - will it be all right?" Jess's voice was little more than a whisper.

"Yes," Adam answered. "A frantic search went on into the night to find a foster mother, and a famous stud has loaned a mare whose foal was born dead. The foal's wounds weren't deep. The owner sounds really nice as she doesn't care what the foal looks like as long as she recovers."

"Why should she care about its looks?" demanded Jess, finding her voice.

"Well, she breeds show ponies," said Adam.

Jess, swallowing hard, asked, "How can we be sure our ponies are safe?"

"We can't," said Susan bluntly. "The attack happened in daylight a few yards from the owner's bungalow. The ponies were in a small paddock. The police couldn't find any clues like footprints or tyre marks."

"Why did it happen?" asked Jess. "Why would anyone do such a vicious thing?"

"The police think it must be someone with a grudge against the owner but she doesn't agree and says she gets on with everyone and Dad's friend David, who is her vet, says she couldn't have enemies. Anyway, a jealous exhibitor wouldn't do such a vicious thing."

"I think you're right, Adam. It's more likely to be a really nasty person who gets kicks from doing terrible things. I wish we could go home and be with the ponies, they're much more important than school." Susan's words expressed the feelings of the other two as the bus turned into the school entrance.

At five-thirty Jess and Marmalade arrived at the Barnes's drive to see only Adam riding, accompanied by Siani.

"Susan's finishing last night's maths," he explained. "She suddenly remembered it's got to be in by tomorrow, and old Plum won't accept late work."

"Glad we don't have her," said Jess. Susan and Alison were welcome to be in Set One maths with the fierce Miss Plumpton.

Marmalade and Pie stepped out eagerly side-by-side. Siani trotted a little way ahead, keeping close to the hedge and glancing back now and then.

For a while the children discussed Sonata's music programme, then Adam said, "High Beeches - where we're going - is a hill-top wood. You'll like it - p'raps it'll remind you of Exmoor."

Perhaps not! thought Jess, but said, "The ponies could do with a climb. I don't want Marmalade to get soft."

About half a mile along the lane they turned right into a huge sloping field, recently cut for silage. After trotting a few yards they squeezed the ponies into canter, keeping perfectly together as they followed the line of the hedge.

"Look, a hare!" cried Adam, as Siani streaked off in futile pursuit.

"They are big!" exclaimed Jess. "I didn't often see them on the moor."

"Funny the way you don't see them with rabbits," commented Adam.

Siani gave up the unequal chase and returned, panting. Watching her now hunting along the hedge bottom, Jess noticed the profusion of flowers: late primroses, celandines, bluebells, campion and bugle. Creamy sprays of hawthorn softened the acid green of young hornbeam hornbeam and beech.

Adam dismounted to open an awkward gate. He let go of Pie to use both hands, and the pony stood like a rock.

"Gosh, he's good," said Jess.

"He's used to it." Adam grinned. "The farmer who owns this field doesn't like having a bridle-path, so he won't look after his gates. I think he deliberately makes it as difficult for us."

He led Pie through the gap then, once Marmalade was safely clear, pushed and lifted the gate back onto the catch, and remounted.

"Shall we canter up to the wood 'til they run out of steam?"

Jess nodded. "They're not too unfit. It won't hurt them."

A hundred yards from the top the ponies slowed to a walk, puffing a little. A fence encircled the towering beeches, with a hunting gate allowing access.

"This doesn't belong to the farmer," said Adam and he expertly opened the gate from the saddle.

"Let's give the ponies a breather then jump some fallen trees," he suggested.

Agreeing happily, Jess looked around at the huge majestic trees and the amazing view over acres and acres of farm and woodland.

"There's Tom's farm," she exclaimed, pointing. "Why do we never see him?"

"He's away at school."

"Does he mind too much?"

"Mind! He loves it. It's a rest cure compared with the holidays. His dad expects him to help on the farm. Look Jess, over there - Lord Connor's woods and you can just see the chimneys of the manor. Down there is Berrywood. The poplars hide the stables."

Jess had to admit that seen from High Beeches this part of Surrey was beautiful. Even Marmalade seemed enthralled with the view. She stood like a statue gazing towards her new home. Then Jess felt a sudden pang of doubt; could she be looking for a glimpse of the moor, even of the sea?

Adam's voice broke into her thoughts. "Come on, let's jump. There are some quite big ones."

He led the way, cantering easily over the smooth trunks, twisting this way and that through the wood.

"Good training for show jumping," he called over his shoulder.

As they turned westwards the sinking sun fired the horizon and, even though they were under the sheltering trees, their eyes were dazzled. One day, Jess thought, I've got to paint this.

"We'll go back through the stables. There's a bridle-path leading to the road," Adam said, and whistled for Siani who came streaking from the heart of the wood.

They rode downhill slowly towards a line of poplars, dark against the pink-washed sky. Jess could see no way through them, but Adam rode straight to a hunting gate right in the middle. They entered a paddock where an aged donkey grazed. He lifted his head and brayed a friendly greeting, which Pie answered with a whicker and Marmalade with an astonished snort. She stood stock still, every muscle, nerve and sinew tense, ready for fight or flight. She was impervious to Jess's aids.

Adam started to laugh but Jess, struggling with a new experience, a totally unresponsive and stubborn Marmalade, was inclined to be cross.

"If you could see her expression," gasped Adam. "She's rolling her eyes..."

"Oh, of course," exclaimed Jess, "she's never seen a donkey before. I s'pose, to her, it may as well be a dinosaur!" She patted the pony to reassure her.

Adam dismounted and led Pie over to the donkey. They rubbed muzzles while Marmalade watched, transfixed, then she gave a snort followed by a long sigh and, relaxing, looked nonchalantly around the paddock.

"She's saying she knew perfectly well it was just a little donkey, only she was taken by surprise," said Adam, laughing. "I bet Pie'd react like that if he saw a red deer." He gently stroked the donkey's long ears. "Isn't he gorgeous?"

Siani certainly thought so as she licked the donkey's muzzle.

"You all seem to know him well," said Jess.

"He comes to stay with us sometimes and helps to keep the grass down. He's an old friend," Adam explained. "He's called Asterix."

"Doesn't your dad worry about ringworm – or is it lungworm?" Jess asked.

"Gosh no. There's so much rubbish talked about it. Sally worms him regularly with all the horses and he's in brilliant condition. It's thought he's in his thirties."

"That's incredible," Jess exclaimed. "I wonder if Sonata will ever look like that."

"Hope not," said Adam, leading Pie over to the gate. "Wouldn't Mrs Carey disown her?"

Jess giggled. "Oh, you know what I mean. Anyway, she had a donkey when she was little. I've seen a photo of her sitting in a wicker basket instead of a saddle."

Adam held the gate open for Jess and Marmalade, who took sly glances over her shoulder but the donkey, unimpressed, was busy grazing again. Mounting Pie, Adam led the way past a Dutch barn and the indoor school into the yard, where Siani suddenly shot forward and took a flying leap into the water trough, immersing herself up to her ears.

"Adam, why don't you stop her? She always does it."

The voice was full of humour and belonged to a slight, fair-haired girl leading a tall bay horse from the indoor school.

"Sorry," called Adam, grinning.

"That's what you always say. Well, it could have been worse - last time she drenched two of my pupils - but my horses don't like drinking dog's hairs and fleas."

"Cheek!" said Adam. "Siani hasn't got fleas. These people are Jess and Marmalade."

"Hullo both of you. I'm Sally as Adam was about to mention. I've heard about you rescuing the old horse. What an amazing story! We had no idea there was still a horse there. And this is Marmalade. What a beautiful pony."

Jess blushed and beamed. What a contrast with her former visit! If Sally had taken the rally it couldn't have been anything but fun. It wouldn't have mattered if Marmalade had stopped at every mirror to admire herself. She looked approvingly at Sally's brown freckled face and kind yellow-green eyes.

"I like your horse. Isn't he huge."

Sally laughed. "He's sixteen-two. He's called Mackie and was my first eventer. I've had him since I was fifteen and now he's our cross-country schoolmaster."

The big, gentle horse whickered as if approving his mistress's words and several horses looking over their half doors answered him.

"I've ridden him," said Adam. "You just sit there and he knows exactly what to do. He's wonderful."

"I hear your father was called out after that terrible attack. It was on the local news and Alison gave me more details. Did you know it's not the first one in this area?"

Shocked the children shook their heads.

"Well, the first one was about a month ago and the horse survived. He's a retired racehorse, just quietly hacked out now and a real family pet. The owner asked for no publicity, afraid there'd be copycat attacks; but now there's been this second one she's talked to the press. It's hard to imagine anyone could be so vicious."

About to reply Adam was cut short by a shout from a nearby loose box.

"Hi, where's Susan? Why isn't she out on Tara?"

The children turned to see Alison carefully balancing a saddle on the door while reaching for the bolt.

"Susan's finishing maths from last night," Adam told her,

"Why didn't she ask me to ride Tara? Linus has been working and I'd have loved to come with you."

There was a tone in Alison's voice that might have worried anyone else, but easygoing Adam didn't seem to notice it.

"I didn't think to suggest it," he said. "Sorry."

Not quite banging the door Alison marched out and into the tack room.

"Oh dear, Ali's a bit put out," said Sally. "Never mind, she'll get over it. Now, I must put this chap in his box and get his supper. Come and see us again, Jess, and I'll introduce you to all the horses."

"Thanks, I'd love that," Jess replied.

Calling 'Goodbye' but getting no reply from Alison the children rode along the drive and into the village.

"We'd better trot, the light's going fast," Jess said.

A little way from Adam's turning they heard the swish of bike tyres, and, peddling furiously, her face nearly as red as her hair, Alison sped by without a glance.

"Oh dear, she does seem upset," said Jess.

"Don't worry, it's not your fault. It's not as if you're riding Tara,' said Adam. 'Ali's often a bit moody; I s'pose it's to do with her dad going off."

Jess was not reassured. All the while Alison had been complaining to Adam her angry gaze had not left Jess's face.

Chapter 7

For days the children felt anxious about their ponies, wondering if they should bring them in at night, which they would hate, or continue with their usual routines but check them very often. They decided on the latter, roping in their parents to help while they were at school.

Pam's sudden, excessive involvement with the horses was unnoticed by Mrs Carey. She was obsessed with the monumental task of having a lift installed. Not a stair lift to spoil her splendid staircase, but a proper lift in a shaft constructed in the unused gunroom. To drown the considerable noise the builders made she listened to very loud music.

"Little does she know her horse is doing the same, only a lot quieter," said Pam.

"I'm jolly glad she's thinking of other things than Sonata," said Jess, who was afraid of revealing the secret to Mrs Carey on her, now, daily visit. She was feeling less warm again towards the old lady and no warmer towards Sam, although she knew, deep down, he could not fairly be blamed for Sonata's condition. When Maggie asked her if she would like to visit him she hesitated, then said she was a bit too busy. At once she felt rather mean, but not enough to change her mind. When Mrs Carey enthused about Sam's amazing progress she experienced a niggling resentment and confided this to Adam.

"No one suggested Sam might have to be put down," she grumbled.

Adam couldn't help smiling but he understood, and said people were always thought to be more important than animals. He considered this was very arrogant and that it would probably bring about the downfall of the human race.

"And not a bad thing," said Jess, grinning. "P'raps the dinosaurs would come back."

With Susan and a friend called Emma, who was not a rider but shared their love of animals, Jess discussed Alison's hostility towards her.

"Oh don't bother about it," said Susan. "She's not talking to Adam if that's any consolation."

"No, it isn't," Jess said, in exasperation. "I don't understand her."

"Don't try," advised Emma. "Some people are a bit moody and Ali's one of them, but when she's in a good mood she's so nice and such fun that the other times don't matter. She's more often really nice than really nasty."

"But why is she so horrid to me? What have I done?"

Susan grinned. "Look, Jess, Ali's a bit jealous. Adam's always been her special friend, or, at least, she thinks so."

"She thinks she goes out with him," said Emma.

"How d'you mean 'goes out with'? Where do they go out?"

Susan and Emma exchanged looks of incredulity, then burst out laughing.

"What's so funny?" Jess demanded.

"Oh you know..." gasped Susan. "They don't go anywhere, they just - go out - it's just an expression."

Jess went scarlet with annoyance and embarrassment. It was not the first time she had felt herself to be a country bumpkin in the company of her new friends.

She said no more about Alison but hoped they would all ride together on Saturday. However, only the twins trotted along the drive at ten o'clock.

"I asked Ali if she could come on Linus, but she's helping Sally at a practice show," explained Susan, but Jess was sure she would have refused anyway.

Twenty minutes later riding over the cross-country fences, Jess forgot all about Alison in the fun of swapping ponies and finding them such good rides in their different ways. Pie was steady and reliable, the sort who would always try his best.

"He's like one of those top showjumpers who, you know, won't refuse unless it's really dangerous to jump," Jess called, and Adam beamed in agreement.

Tara was altogether different. As ticklish as a thoroughbred, she had to be ridden firmly but tactfully; a wrong or inconsiderate move and she would fizz up like a shaken coke can. Jess realised how well Susan rode. It surprised her for she thought Adam was the quiet, tactful rider but, clearly, Susan was just as good. The twins were enthusiastic about Marmalade.

"She rides like a much bigger pony," said Susan.

"She makes me think of a little war horse, ready to charge at the lightest touch," said Adam. "Aren't we lucky all having such good ponies."

He leaned forward to give Pie a hug, and, grinning, Susan started to sing:

"Bye, bye Miss American Pie..."

They were all singing at the tops of their voices as they clattered into the yard at The Elms.

"What a racket!" said Maggie, laughing. "Have you been to the pub?"

"Maggie!" Jess's tone was shocked. "As if we..." Her voice tailed off into laughter. "You certainly stopped at the pub! Those are cans of beer in your basket!"

"Is Maggie a dipso?" muttered Adam so only Jess could hear.

Maggie held up a small can for all to see.

"Stout!" exclaimed Adam.

"Yes, for Mrs Carey."

"Crikey, so she's a dipso."

Ignoring Adam, Maggie said, "She fancies a drop with her lunch to build her strength up and she thinks Sonata should have some too."

"It'll put her off her food altogether. It's disgusting," Jess said, in horror.

Maggie unbuckled her bike basket.

"It won't be her first taste of stout. I don't doubt she and Sam shared a bottle in the old days."

Nodding in agreement Susan pointed out that many racehorses were given stout and beer.

"That's right," Maggie agreed. "Let's just try her with a tiny drop to keep Mrs C. happy. Ask your dad what he thinks... Oh, yes, I nearly forgot, he's coming to see her on Monday."

The children exchanged anxious glances.

"Should we tell him about the music?" asked Susan.

"No, it might influence his judgement."

"Adam, of course it wouldn't, Dad's far too professional for that."

"Then why bother to ask? Anyway, it's up to Jess to decide. You're such a know-all, Susan."

Pam's appearance at the back door forestalled an argument.

"What d'you think, Mum?" asked Jess, explaining the problem.

"Well - we'll wait 'til the examination is over, then I'll explain what you've been doing. Now, shall I hold Tara and Pie so you can visit Sonata?"

The twins dismounted and disappeared into the stable. Maggie and Pam, with Jess's cautious agreement decided to pour a few drops of stout on the old mare's lunch.

"We don't want her dancing to the music," said Maggie, going indoors.

Pie smeared Pam's bare arm with green froth.

"This pony's been eating with his bit in. Naughty Adam. Did you have a good ride?"

"Brill: we swapped ponies," said Jess from under the saddle flap.

"Do tell Mrs Carey about it. She wants all of you to have a picnic supper in her room tonight. There's a film on television about the wild horses of The Camargue. She thought it would be fun for you all to watch it together."

Jess scowled. She didn't want Mrs Carey muscling in on her friendships.

"I don't expect they'll want to. They can watch it at home."

Pam frowned. She put a hand on Marmalade's head collar while Jess removed her saddle.

"I must ask them, Jess. Poor Mrs Carey is really quite lonely."

"Oh, come on, Mum, she has loads of friends - people are always ringing up."

"Yes, I know, but they are all as old as she is, and can't get about easily. I think she feels very out of touch and wants a bit of variety. She's longing to have the lift so she can get out a bit, particularly to visit Sam. Since she's been a bit better she's been really frustrated with being indoors all the time."

"She only feels better 'cause you persuaded her doctor to change her treatment. I hope she realises that."

"I'm sure she does, Jess, but it is what I'm here for." Pam's tone was unusually reproving.

The twins came out looking cheerful.

"She's brighter, I'm sure she is," said Susan. "And her coat's like velvet."

"She looked round at us as if she was saying, 'Hullo'," Adam enthused.

Pam told them about Mrs Carey's invitation and, later, they rang to say they'd love to come.

Jess had to admit that the picnic supper was a success. Mrs Carey's effusive praise for her care of Sonata embarrassed her a bit. She cringed to hear that she had saved Sonata's life, and blushed furiously when Adam caught her eye and gave an exaggerated wink. It was generous of him not to suggest his father too had played a part in Sonata's improvement. The twins and Mrs Carey got on really well; in fact, Jess had never heard Adam talk so much.

She was allowed to show them over the house and was amazed when they lingered in front of dark oil paintings that Jess, the artist, had dismissed as dismal beyond words.

"I bet the house was quite nice once," Susan commented. "I mean with all those dust sheets removed."

Just before they left Adam mentioned the latest Pony Club newsletter. Jess was aware that hers had arrived and was tucked behind the kitchen clock, waiting to be opened – or not.

"You'll be at the rally at half-term, won't you?" asked Adam. "Bradders is expecting you and Marmalade."

"Oh, you must come," said Susan. "You'll miss all the fun if you don't."

Jess frowned. "I don't want to talk about it," she said, but the twins wouldn't let the matter drop.

At their house the next day they began again and, overhearing from the kitchen and sorry for Jess because she was outnumbered, Lin interrupted, "Jess has a lot to think of with Sonata still poorly. Give the poor girl some space. I don't suppose you've any idea of the responsibility she has."

And it was to the twins' credit that they did not reveal the extent of their involvement and just exchanged conspiratorial winks.

"Dad's seeing Sonata tomorrow, isn't he?" Adam asked, in an innocent tone. " Hope he'll find her much, much better."

Rushing in from school on Monday, Jess was instantly deflated to find the kitchen empty. Against the kettle was a piece of card on which Pam had printed in red felt tip:

SORRY - UPSTAIRS. BULLETIN: ENCOURAGING PROGRESS!!
MUSIC THERAPY WILL BE FREELY PRESCRIBED!!

After reading that it was impossible to concentrate on homework, especially with Susan ringing twice to suggest playing rock tapes, leading gradually to Heavy Metal.

"Sonata's ready for more stimulation," enthused Jess, after repeating Susan's suggestion and nearly hugging the breath out of her mother.

Gasping, Pam replied, "Well, she won't get her hour's grooming every afternoon if I have to endure that! Anyway, I think she's acquired a taste for Elgar."

Jess laughed but a minute later when Mrs Carey's bell rang, her elation evaporated. "Mum, you've only just come down."

"It's not for me; Mrs Carey said she'd ring if she wanted you to go up. John didn't tell her about the music therapy. He said it was your story to tell. Why don't you go up and tell her all about it?"

Jess hesitated. "It was really Adam's idea, then we were all involved."

"Well, you can tell her that. Go on, Jess, she's in such a good mood and much more positive about Sonata, although I had to be brutally honest and admit she hates stout on her feeds!"

If only Alison would be friends again. Whenever Jess walked towards her at school she turned away, and, at the end of another week, Jess knew there was no chance of her joining their rides. Nevertheless, there had been plenty of good happenings, such as Sonata licking her bowl clean so that, cautiously, Jess increased her feeds. She appeared to enjoy her surroundings when she joined Marmalade in the paddock on warm days.

"You seem at a loose end," observed Pam, finding Jess gazing moodily out of the kitchen window. "Aren't you riding this morning?"

"Not 'til after lunch. The twins have to go to the dentist."

"Then be a dear and post a letter for me, will you? If I ask Maggie to do it on her way home it'll miss the collection. It's a birthday card for Liz's mum."

"Oh gosh, did you include me?"

"Yes, of course. I had a chat with her on Wednesday. She rang to say she'd visited Daddy's grave and it's looking beautiful, covered with grape hyacinths, forget-me-nots and primroses - imagine the scent. And she's so pleased you and Liz chat often. Here's the card. Will you go on your bike?"

Jess nodded and put the card in her pocket.

"Be careful, darling."

"Mum, I'm not five."

"Nor are drivers, Jess, but sometimes they behave as if they are."

Arriving safely at the village shop Jess found there was a queue at the post office counter. While she waited she glanced at the rows of magazines and decided to treat herself and Pam. What would her mother like she wondered, but her attention was diverted by a conversation going on at the glass window.

"There's been trouble at the stables. Police cars there since early morning."

"A break-in, d'you mean?"

"Don't know. Must be a crime or the police wouldn't be there, would they?"

The elderly speaker moved forward to collect her pension money. Jess stood behind her.

"Hope it hasn't been - well, you know..." She glanced round at Jess, than leaned forward, her face close to the window. Jess's straining ears could not catch her words, but she saw the expression of horror on the postmistress's face.

The old lady took ages putting every note separately into her wallet then, counting coins into her purse, she asked, "Not keeping you, dear, am I?"

Jess shook her head hypocritically, willing her to move.

At last, having safely stamped and posted the birthday card, Jess stood beside her bike wondering what to do. If there'd been some trouble at the stables maybe she could be of use. She felt a strong, sudden compulsion to go there.

The front yard was empty. There was no Saturday morning bustle with children and ponies busy in every direction. Only three boxes were occupied yet there was no sign of lessons in progress. Jess propped her bike against a wall and was about to walk to the rear yard when she caught a glimpse of bright red curls. Swiftly she crossed to a far loose box and looked over the half door. Alison was shaking out fresh straw with a pitchfork. She looked up startled, and stared at Jess with a strange, bewildered look.

Shocked, Jess was unable to speak. Alison's face was streaked with dust and tears. Her eyes were red-rimmed and puffy and, as she stood there silently, fresh tears trickled down her cheeks.

Chapter 8

Jess unlatched the door and hurried across to her. "Ali - what's wrong? Has something happened to - Linus?"

"N - no - He's in the p - paddock." Alison had difficulty speaking. "It's M – Mackie - lovely old Mackie... He's d - dead."

Jess put her arms around her and was grateful that she was not pushed away.

"Mackie was – stabbed early this morning - in his box..."

Horrified, Jess hugged her and felt her own tears running down her face. "Oh no, that dear old horse. Poor Sally."

"Her parents are here. They came at once. Lots of parents are mucking out in the other yard..." Alison's voice broke into sobs. For minutes the girls hugged each other for comfort then, recovering a little, Alison sat down on a bale of straw and was able to talk.

"John Barnes has been here, and the police. All the students are so upset...Too upset to do much work."

"Right then, I'll stay and help. We'll work together, shall we?"

Mackie's box was padlocked. John Barnes and the police could do no more. From the little paddock came the sad braying of the bewildered little donkey, whose friend would never join him again.

For more than two hours the girls worked with parents and all but the youngest pupils, fortified by mugs of tea and sandwich lunches, brought round by one of the mothers who insisted that everyone should have a break at half past one.

Suddenly, Jess remembered she had only gone out to post a birthday card. What would her mother be thinking? That she'd had an accident?

"No mobile phone? Well, ring your mother from the office. Sally won't mind in the circumstances," the kindly mother suggested; so Jess rang the house number, which was different from Mrs Carey's, and there was no reply so she left a message.

"She's always up with Mrs Carey," she complained, "and I don't know the other number. I bet she hasn't even missed me."

"Well, come with me to Laburnum Lodge," suggested Alison. "John said I could take Asterix there to be with Tara and Pie. I'm going to lead him from my bike."

Together they went to fetch the donkey who was waiting at the gate.

"Don't you like Mrs Carey?" asked Alison, putting the donkey's head collar on, gently easing it over his great, furry ears.

"Oh sometimes - well, most of the time, but she works Mum really hard. I bet she could look after six patients really well in the time she's looking after Mrs Carey. There are people you just can't like all the time even though you call them a friend."

As the words came out Jess wondered, in dismay, what Alison might make of them. She'd gone a bit pink and avoided looking at Jess while she put Asterix on the nearside of her bike, and, wobbling a little, set off. Jess drew ahead and waved down a driver coming along much too fast. He looked surprised, then grinned and waved at her.

The twins were grooming their ponies but they rushed outside to greet Asterix and put him in the spare box next to Tara, so they could have a chat. Both were terribly upset but Susan's grief had turned to anger and she longed to wreak vengeance on Mackie's killer.

"I'd plunge a knife into him if I caught him. If the police catch him I bet he'll just be fined. He should be given life imprisonment, after all, he *is* a murderer. Dad says it's the same person each time - they're sure of that although he doesn't leave any clues."

Adam then supplied the information that mattered and forestalled Alison's difficult question. "Remember, Dad said it was instantaneous - an expert job."

Alison nodded gratefully.

"Are you going to ride with us?" asked Susan. "If you don't want to go back for Linus you can have Tara."

"Or Marmalade," offered Jess, not to be outdone. "I can ride tomorrow and I've masses of homework to catch up with."

Alison hesitated, "I'm - not sure that I want to ride."

"Oh do, Ali," Adam urged. "It'll do you good. In a way it's even beastlier for you, knowing Sally and Mackie so well. Go on - you can have Pie."

At that Alison almost laughed. "I can't ride all three. Tell you what, let's all swap around. It's dry enough to take a bike through the woods, but first I must go home and tell Granny what's happening."

"And I'll have to dash to get Marmalade ready," said Jess. "See you in about half-an-hour."

After Alison had sped off Susan looked at Jess curiously.

"How did you two make it up?" she asked, and Jess told the whole story from going to the post office.

"Poor Ali," said Susan, when she finished. "And even more poor Sally. Dad said she was in a terrible state and her doctor came and gave her a sedative. He said she'll probably be too woozy to do anything much this weekend."

"Then let's all go and help tomorrow," said Jess. "She needs all the help she can get. Right, see you soon."

Within days a security system was installed at Berrywood Stables. A light came on in each of the yards the moment anyone approached, even a prowling cat. Every loose box was wired up to an alarm bell.

The twins wanted their parents to install a similar system but their father pointed out that they already had security lights and a burglar alarm, and anything more would be far too expensive.

"Oh, yes it's all right for the house to be protected but it doesn't matter about the ponies," said Susan, angrily. "Fat lot of use that is."

Jess was equally disappointed with Mrs Carey's response. Appalled by the attack, she suggested that Sonata and Marmalade should be locked in the stable at night. And she would allow Pam more time off to visit them frequently during the day. Even the gardener was interviewed and asked to be especially vigilant in these difficult times.

"Not for nothing was she an army wife," said Maggie, amused.

Still, Jess felt these measures were inadequate but derived some comfort from the knowledge that only a sledgehammer would effect entry to the stable at night. Marmalade, however, took a dim view of her nightly confinement and, one evening, refused to be caught for the first time ever.

At midnight, too anxious to sleep, Jess crept downstairs, pulled overalls over her pyjamas and went out to entice Marmalade with a snack of apple slices and sugar lumps. Pleased at such an unexpected visit Marmalade whickered, hurried across and lowered her nose into the feed bowl. Jess slipped the head collar on with expert deftness. She stood stroking the pony's neck and glancing around the moonlit paddock, but it was Marmalade who spotted the badger. She lifted her head abruptly, ears pricked, and following the direction of her gaze Jess picked out the beautiful, distinctive markings on its head. Not thirty yards away, it was unperturbed by their presence and ambled towards the hedge scratching with its nose for something tasty to eat.

The memory of her first sight of badgers flashed into Jess's mind; it was on her sixth birthday. She had sat shivering with excitement, not cold, leaning against her father while, unseen but overheard, the mysterious, wonderful creatures lumbered about, grunting and playing. Then, like a great silver disk, the moon slipped into a clear patch of sky and a large badger family appeared before them as if by magic.

Safely back in her room, her mission accomplished, Jess set her alarm clock knowing that now her mind was at rest she would sleep like a log.

A few days later in Set One maths Susan stretched her arms across her desk, put her head on them and fell fast asleep. Almost to the minute in Set Two, Adam's head slumped onto his shoulder and he gave a loud, long snore. On Wednesday, in double science, his head fell onto a Bunsen burner and his hair was slightly singed; an hour later the Deputy Head was on the telephone to Lin Barnes.

Later, riding alone because the twins had been banned for a week, Alison and Jess considered why their parents had made such a fuss about their nightly patrols around the paddocks and stable.

"It's not at all how I'd expect them to react," said Alison. "John is as upset as anyone about the killings. Twice he's been one of the first at the scene of the crime."

Jess agreed. "You'd think he'd be jolly pleased his kids care about their ponies so much, but, you know, I can't always depend on Mum to react how I expect her to."

Alison narrowed her eyes against the lowering sun. She glanced behind her then, in almost a whisper, said, "D'you think John has inside information?"

Jess was startled and gave a sudden shiver.

Alison continued. "He was on the spot even before the police. He may have seen something that only he and the police know about."

Jess stared at her, intrigued. "You could be right. Doctors get to murders pretty early and give vital information to the police. It's the same kind of situation only the victim was a horse."

"Yes," said Alison in a bitter tone. "The only difference is the police can't be bothered. They haven't set up an incident room, or made door-to-door enquiries. I bet they haven't even done as John suggested, visiting slaughter houses and butchers - and even vets."

They rode in silent, angry commiseration for a while then Alison suggested, "Let's go back through Berrywood and I can show you Mackie's grave."

"Is Mackie buried in the little paddock he shared with Asterix?"

"Yes, a beech tree has been planted on his grave, protected by a little fence."

Riding through the rear yard Jess noticed Mackie's box was still shut. Poor Sally could still not bear to see another horse in there.

"I won't come down to Laburnum with you and Tara," said Jess. "The twins have to go to bed early so we won't see them."

"Okay, but I've got an idea. I'll talk about it tomorrow at break when we're all together - just the four of us."

Alison's words intrigued Jess all the way home.

The next morning, hurrying to catch the school bus, they came back to her. Then, at break she was frustrated when Alison said, "It's too public to talk about it here, so let's meet for about half-an-hour before doing our homework."

And so at four-thirty they were all sitting at the dining-room table with only Siani, Marmite and Magic party to the discussion.

"You've got a detailed map of this area, haven't you, Adam?"

"Think so, Ali. D'you want it?"

"Yes, it's vital."

Adam fetched it from his bedroom and opened it out on the table. Instantly, Magic jumped on to it from Jess's knee and stretched out. Gently, Adam scooped her to one side. Marmite gave a jealous bark and leapt on to Adam's knee, but was content to sit there with his forepaws on the table.

"Thank you, Marmite; can we get on?" asked Alison.

"You can if you address him as Mister Chairman," said Adam.

"Not 'Mister'," interposed Susan, "it's chairperson, sexist beast."

"Oh, do shut, you two. This is a serious meeting. Adam, d'you mind if I mark the map? I'll use pencil."

"No, that's okay."

Fascinated, all eyes were on Alison as she underlined the names of three villages, one being Berrywood. Then she rummaged in her schoolbag for a ruler and pair of compasses.

"Better not make a hole in the table," she suggested, and waited while Adam slid a tablemat under the map. Then she drew a circle around the three names.

"I see," commented Susan, "they're within a small radius."

"Not more than five miles between villages," agreed Adam.

"Right. No clues were found, such as tyre marks, and no strange cars have been spotted, so the killer could be very local and getting about on foot."

"What about footprints then?" asked Susan.

"Wouldn't show on dry ground whereas tyre marks do. I've been looking out for things like that."

"Crikey, Ali, no wonder you're in Set One for everything," said Adam.

Ignoring him, Alison continued, "Only something heavy leaves marks so we can rule out a car."

"What about a bike?" asked Jess.

"Hmm... Probably would leave signs but I don't think we can be certain."

Adam put his finger on a hamlet a few miles away.

"Nearest slaughter house; about seven miles from us and further from the other villages. Quite a long way to go on foot when the whole area is bristling with horses."

"Yes, but he won't live in a slaughter house, he'll just work there."

"Right," said Susan briskly. "Suppose the killer lives within this small radius, how do we find him? We can't go around knocking on doors asking if the horse killer lives there."

"Of course we can't, but the police could." Alison gave her a paint-stripping look.

Her father coming in looking for the evening newspaper forestalled Susan's response.

"Not geography homework?" he remarked.

Adam grinned and was about to fold the map when Alison plunged in. "We think the killer lives within this area."

John Barnes stared at the map for a moment. "Why?"

Taken aback, Alison explained their reasons.

"Yes, it's a logical assumption," he agreed. "It all makes excellent sense."

"Then why aren't the police doing something?" demanded Susan.

"How do we know they aren't?" her father replied, picking Magic up.

"Well, no one's been arrested. In a murder hunt you hear about people helping the police with their enquiries. Then sometimes they're released. We haven't even heard that."

"I know, but the reality is that the police don't regard these acts as murder. They won't be hauling in suspects on slight suspicion; they'll want proof, or near proof."

"Then they'll wait forever, and the killer will probably get away with it. I bet we could find him."

Susan sounded both angry and tearful. Her father sat down at the table with Magic on his lap, purring. Looking unusually serious, he said, "I was party to the discussion at the killings. The police agree that it's the work of the same person each time, and he has skill and knowledge..."

"He - why not she?" demanded Adam. "Anyway, we know all that."

"Just be patient. It's important because it narrows the search. Not only has this person unusual knowledge of horse anatomy, but must have super-human strength. I'm taller than average and pretty strong, but I couldn't kill a horse with the accuracy of this person."

"So what does that tell the police? That he comes from a circus or is a boxer?" Susan's tone was full of exasperation.

"That's not a bad idea. He may be someone who does weight training, or boxing, or one of the martial arts. He may have trained in the armed forces."

"So are the police looking at fitness clubs?" asked Adam.

"I don't know. I hope so."

"Can't you find out, Dad?"

"I can ask but I doubt if they'll give me a blow-by-blow account of the investigation so far. I'd probably get very short shrift if I expected that."

Adam looked crestfallen.

"Could you talk to the press?" Alison suggested. "You know the sort of thing - `local vet puts his ideas...'"

"Alison, I'd probably do more harm than good. If they've got their eye on a suspect they won't want him warned off."

"Why not?" said Jess. "It might stop another killing."

John looked at his watch then, gently putting Magic on the floor, stood up.

"I must start surgery. I'm sorry if I've made you feel worse. Believe me, we're not discussing a character from an adventure story; the police think he could be very dangerous."

As the door closed behind him, Susan swore quietly but vehemently. "So that's the end of our amateur sleuthing. That's how Dad regards it."

"It needn't be," Alison's voice was positive and excited. "I've still got an idea..."

Adam groaned and pretended to collapse. Alison ignored him.

"We'll write to the police putting down all the things we think they should be doing and looking for."

"They won't take it seriously. They'll send a polite reply and do nothing," said Susan.

"Then we'll write to the local paper as if it's from grown-ups. I'll type it on the computer."

"I'll sign it, Alison," said Adam stoutly.

"What if the killer reads it and takes revenge?" Jess suggested.

"We can ask them not to print our names, or not in full, and I'll give my address as we haven't any ponies there," said Alison stoutly.

"Won't your granny mind?"

"No, Jess, of course not. She'll support us."

"Right, let's get on with it then," enthused Susan. "Doesn't doing something make you feel so much better?"

Chapter 9

"Hi - wait for me."

The cavalcade of Susan, Adam and Alison on bikes and Jess on Marmalade, slowed so that Tom Latcham could catch up. True as their word, the children had worked hard to show the pony at her best. They had removed enough woolly coat to stuff a mattress. The sheen on her mane and tail was largely attributable to Brilliantine (borrowed by Adam from his parents' bathroom). Her small hooves gleamed and her tack was as pristine as, unusually, were Jess's jodhpur boots. Both pony and rider were difficult to fault.

Tom's bike drew level with Adam's. His face was pink from his exertions.

"Have you seen the letter about the horse attacks? It's in the local rag. Mum spotted it just as I was leaving. She read it through the kitchen window - that's why I'm late."

Tom paused, out of breath. Jess trotting briskly in the lead, heard none of this; so Alison pedalled vigorously alongside relaying the news.

"It's from four horse lovers - names supplied but not printed - for security I s'pose."

"Go on, Tom," Susan's face was a picture of genuine curiosity.

"Well - it's asking questions - mainly, like, have the police interviewed slaughtermen, butchers and vets? Have they considered the type of person the attacker might be? Someone of superhuman strength - into weight lifting or wrestling - that sort of thing. Mum said if the police haven't done all these things, they should be ashamed."

Struggling to keep a serious face, and not show his delight that the letter had been printed, Adam asked, "Does it suggest the killer might be a local person?"

"Oh yes, because of there not being vehicle tyre marks, and the attacks being within a small radius."

Although as pleased and excited as the others, Jess's overwhelming feeling was of anxiety about the ordeal ahead. Three cars packed with waving Pony Club members had passed by in the last few minutes. When the children reached Berrywood Stables their talk was still about the letter, but Jess was no longer hearing. At a glance she saw at least forty members of assorted ages and sizes. She drew Marmalade up, dismounted and stared around in dismay.

Mrs Bradshaw bore down on them in flagship fashion with a welcoming beam on her large, round face.

"Oh, you look splendid! How hard you must have worked. Marmalade is a credit to you."

"Thanks, but to all of us really. They've all helped to get her ready."

"Then, well done all of you. Now we'll put her in this box until we need her."

"Well, what was the rally like?" asked Pam, carefully putting a warm fruit cake on a wire tray in the middle of the table.

Jess who was flipping through one of Adam's skate board magazines, looked up with a broad smile and said, "It was brilliant."

Pam sat down. "You actually enjoyed it?"

"Yes, we all did - well almost all. Some of the older ones giggled a lot and tried to slip out to have a smoke. Can you imagine it, Mum - in a stable? Anyhow, they got into big trouble and had to sit in the front between Bradders and Trotters. Then Tom came in really late, although he arrived with us. He made everyone get up so he could sit next to Ali..."

"Yes, darling, but what about the talk from the famous judge. What did he think of Marmalade?"

"Oh, Mum, he loved her. We had slides and a talk about the nine native breeds. D'you know Highland ponies can carry dead stags - though why they have to be shot I can't imagine - and Shetland ponies carry panniers of seaweed 'cause lots of native ponies still work. I'm glad they don't go down the mines any more – well, there aren't any. The judge mentioned that and one really little kid started to cry."

"Oh dear." Pam put a cup of tea in front of Jess, decided she couldn't wait for the cake to grow cold and cut two large slices.

"This is brilliant Mum," said Jess with her mouth full. She swallowed hard, took a gulp of tea and continued, "I was a bit fed up by the end of the slides 'cause all we saw of Exmoor ponies were little dots in the distance on Dunkery. Then we all went outside and Marmalade was really pleased to see us. She was so good, Mum. She was taking it all in of course, as she stood like a rock while Major Saunders talked about her. He was really interesting and got everyone talking. Ali knew heaps - all about Exmoors being ancient chariot ponies and being here before we broke off from the Continent. D'you know, that was only about ten thousand years ago."

"Goodness, that's nothing considering the age of the earth." Pam poured more tea.

"And an older girl knew about the large cavities in the skull so air is warmed up before it reaches the lungs."

"That's impressive. How much did you know?"

"Oh, all of it, but I didn't say anything. It wouldn't have been fair, would it? I mean, I should know a lot about my own pony. Mr. Cox's little girl knew about toad eye and the snow chute at the top of the tail. Major

Saunders thinks the toad eye was to frighten enemies such as wolves."

"Well, there were wolves on Exmoor, Jess. King John kept a pack of wolf hounds on the moor but I've no idea when they died out. Perhaps we could do a bit of research."

"Major Saunders asked me all about Marmalade's breeding, Mum. He gave me his card."

Jess rummaged in her pocket and handed the card to Pam.

"Oh yes. He's a very well-known breeder. His Exmoor stud is famous."

"He said would we give him first refusal if we ever sell her, Mum. As if we would! But he was really nice and, afterwards, everyone made a great fuss of Marmalade. Susan said they were creeps as they'd been so rude about her in the past but I didn't care as Marmalade really enjoyed herself."

Jess did not add that Annette had rather spoiled things by flinging her arm around Marmalade's neck and then saying, "She is a lovely pony. What a pity she doesn't jump."

A few days into the second half of the term, Jess announced her newly-formed and surprising resolution: to turn Marmalade into an all-round Pony Club pony.

"What changed your mind? Was it everyone being so nice about Marmalade at the rally?"

As Susan seldom altered her opinion about anyone, or changed her mind about anything, there was a note of incredulity in her voice.

Jess swallowed a mouthful of break-time biscuit and explained, "Well - it was partly that, but what really decided me was that awful Annette Wadham-Smith saying 'What a pity she doesn't jump'! Then I thought about all the things she can do, and it seemed awful to waste her, specially as she's a rare breed."

While the others were considering this, Susan said, "You'll have to concentrate on show jumping and dressage, that's obvious."

"I know," Jess said. "I'll need masses of help and - will you all help me?"

There was an affirmative chorus. Even Alison had lifted her head from the music score she had been studying intently.

"We could all work together. It'd be fun. Maybe we could have group dressage lessons with Sally."

Susan did not take kindly to this suggestion. "That's a silly idea, Alison, considering Jess and Marmalade are beginners at dressage."

Adam winked at Alison and, grinning, she returned to her music score.

"Of course I realise I'll be starting from scratch," said Jess. "I only know about dressage from books, and you all know heaps more than I do. I've never tried to ride a dressage test."

"No hass," said Adam. "If Pie and I (sorry!) can do it, anyone can."

"Jess may want to do rather better than you and Pie," said Susan crushingly. "We may as well try to do this properly with the one-day-event at the start of the holidays coming up. How about starting this evening instead of going for a ride? We can use our jumps at home and mark out an arena in the flatter paddock."

"Can't tonight." Alison glanced up again. "Gran and I are having supper with some friends of hers. I don't mind if you start without me."

"Okay, the sooner the better, specially as it's rained a bit so the ground won't be too hard..."

The end-of-break bell forestalled further discussion but plans progressed during the day, culminating in the confiscation of a note passing from Adam to Jess. Glancing at it young Mr Carter said that Adam's enthusiasm for geometry did him credit, but the subject of the moment was algebra. As he dropped the diagram of a dressage arena into the wastepaper bin he was bemused that his words had reduced the miscreants to a state of helplessness.

Jess leapt off the school bus and ran down the drive calling to Marmalade and Sonata, but only the former trotted smartly to the gate to get her customary polo mint. How odd that Sonata was not outside on a sunny afternoon? With a feeling of unease, Jess turned into the stable yard to find her mother and John Barnes in serious discussion. Her schoolbag slipped unheeded onto the cobbles.

"Mum, is something wrong? Is it Sonata? Has something happened to her?"

It was John who answered in his quiet, kindly way. "Don't look so worried. She's just got a touch of colic. I've rather been expecting it."

He put his medical bag in the back of his car beside the gentle Siani, who licked his face then put a proprietary paw on the bag.

"Is it something I've done wrong?" Jess asked.

"No, no, you've looked after her wonderfully. Your mother has described her diet and how much she's been having and I can't find any fault there. You've resisted increasing her food too quickly and that wasn't easy, I'm sure. I think you've done a marvellous job, both of you. The trouble is the gut can be permanently damaged by starvation, so it never copes efficiently again. If that's the case then I'm afraid bouts of colic are inevitable. I hope it will just be a 'one-off' with Sonata."

He gave Jess's arm a sympathetic squeeze and said he'd be back after evening surgery.

"Oh, please tell Susan and Adam I shan't be schooling Marmalade after all. I want to stay with Sonata," Jess said, suddenly remembering their arrangement.

Followed by her mother she entered Sonata's box and stroked the old mare's neck. She gave the quietest whicker which brought a great lump to Jess's throat.

"She will be all right, won't she?" she asked in an unsteady voice.

"John is hopeful, Jess. He's given her an injection and a drench and, already, she's stopped twisting round looking at her tummy, and trying to paw with a hind leg. The effect was almost instantaneous. He says we caught it very early; so there really is every chance she'll get better, but the real problem is whether she'll keep getting it, as he explained to you."

Jess rubbed damp eyes against Sonata's mane. "What can we do now to help her?"

"We mustn't let her lie down, so we'll have to watch her carefully."

"I'll stay here with her, Mum. I can sleep in the next box."

"I don't think that will be necessary, but we are going to have to look at her about every quarter of an hour through the night. Mrs Carey has asked Maggie to sleep in so I can be free."

"Mum, let me stay up. You work really hard; you need your sleep."

"Well, come in and change and have your tea, and we'll work something out."

Retrieving her schoolbag, Jess followed Pam indoors.

"I thought the killer had struck, Mum."

"Yes, I was afraid you'd have a shock. I'm glad the people who wrote that letter didn't have their names and addresses printed." She was looking at Jess quizzically.

"You've guessed, haven't you, Mum?"

"Yes, and so have Lin and John Barnes. It was all four of you?"

"Yes. You're not cross?"

"No, of course not. Rather proud in fact, and I agree with all the points you made. You may have put the attacker off his stroke. Obviously, you all felt very strongly that you had to do something. You haven't much faith in the police, have you?"

Jess hesitated. "I don't think they do as much for animals as people, but maybe they're not allowed to. I expect some of them care a lot."

She took plates, cups and saucers from the dresser and put them on the table. Pam put bread into the toaster, then lifted a newly baked fruit cake out of a tin. Jess eyed it ravenously.

"You're very like Daddy," Pam told her. "He would have had to do something. He didn't care if he took risks or made himself unpopular."

Jess spread a slice of toast with butter and Marmite.

"We were lucky having Daddy, weren't we?"

Pam was looking out of the window, watching swallows darting over the stable roof.

"Yes - very lucky. He knew what was really important in life."

She cut a slice of cake for Jess and poured the tea.

Jess's throat did not hurt now when she talked about her father, or only sometimes. She liked to talk about him; somehow it made him seem not so very far away.

"Mummy, d'you think he knows about us being here, and about Sonata?"

Pam passed her a cup of tea.

"I like to think so."

"Mum, it's difficult understanding - about Heaven. I mean, I want to be sure it's there but, well, it's difficult."

"Yes - I know. That's the hard part, but I suppose that's what's meant by having Faith; being prepared to believe without needing proof."

"Well... I want there to be a Heaven so I can see Daddy and all the grandparents, and my guinea pig again."

"And Marmalade's dam," Pam added, smiling. She glanced at the big kitchen clock. "Any minute now Mrs Carey's bell will ring. I'm very late with her tea."

Jess's expression changed to one of resentment. As ever, she saw far less of her mother than Mrs Carey did. They hardly ever had time to talk about things - important things.

Noticing, Pam said, "I'm sorry, darling, but I must get her tea ready and we need to sort out how we're going to care for Sonata."

In the end she agreed that Jess could stay up until midnight, then she would take over and Jess would go to bed. She would do her homework at the kitchen table as usual, frequently checking Sonata. John Barnes returned and fixed an infra red lamp in place of the ordinary light bulb above the old mare's head.

"We use them for lambs, or any sick or weakly animals - much better than piling on more rugs. Now let's have a look at you, old lady."

He stood looking for a minute, then checked her pulse and temperature.

"Know what they should be?"

"Uhm - pulse 36 to 42, temperature 100 to 100.5 Fahrenheit, about 38 Centigrade."

"Good girl. Pity Mrs Trotman isn't here. Well, there's not much to worry about. Her pulse was racing when she was so distressed but she really seems to have improved. If she were a young horse I'd say she was well on the way to recovery, but I don't think we should take any chances with such an old lady. Has she had anything to drink?"

"Yes, she's had a few sips. She loves slightly warm water."

"Good, she can go on drinking, but no food until she's passed whatever's in her tum. I'll come back before morning surgery but if she becomes very restless, or there's any worrying change, call me at once. I had great difficulty preventing Adam and Susan coming; they wanted to share the night watch but she's better off with people she knows."

"That was really kind of them. Mum and I have worked it out that one of us will check on her regularly. What should we do if she tries to lie down?"

"It may seem mean but she really should stay on her feet. If she tries hard to get down you'll have to throw every rug on her, and walk her about outside. And don't forget, ring me if you're worried."

Greatly reassured Jess went indoors to find Maggie serving up cottage pie for supper.

"This will help you to keep warm if you have to stay out with her."

They sat at the kitchen table eating, having dispatched Pam to rest with strict instructions from Maggie, endorsed by Jess, not to move until midnight. Pam's parting words were, "If you hear anyone moving about come indoors immediately and raise the alarm."

"She thinks the attacker might appear," said Jess grinning. "Honestly! He's not likely to hang around with lights on and someone about. Anyway, I think Sonata's music would put him off."

"Depends what it is." Maggie laughed.

"Very quiet Brahms at present," said Jess, "but, I meant, he'd probably think it was a radio. Maggie, I wanted to stay up all night but Mum wouldn't hear of it. I need my sleep, she said. As if it matters at a time like this."

Maggie chuckled and spooned a second helping onto Jess's plate.

"You do need your sleep - more than us old folk and I'll see your mum has an easy time tomorrow. Mrs Carey is doing so much more for herself; goodness knows what gallivanting she'll get up to once that lift is working."

"Was she very active when she was young?"

"Goodness, yes. If she wasn't riding she was doing something else with the horses or helping at the Pony Club. It was the same with the Colonel. I think they both needed to be busy all the time after their son was killed."

"Was he very young, Maggie?"

"Twenty-two and killed in action. He was in his dad's old regiment. Such a wicked waste. You've seen all the lovely photos of him – from babyhood onwards? Good. Now, duck, there's a nice treacle pudding to fill up the corners."

After Maggie had settled Mrs Carey for the night and gone to bed herself, Jess had an hour of feeling very much alone. She had done her homework and washed up, interspersed with frequent visits to the stable. Unfortunately, Marmalade thought the visits were for her benefit. She whickered a greeting every time and moved noisily about in her box. Jess wondered if she should move her further away from Sonata but suddenly felt too tired to bother. Anyway, Sonata seemed peaceful even though she looked awful. Surely the hollows above her eyes hadn't been so deep, or her neck so thin? Hadn't she been improving? Now she seemed desperately tired, as if she'd been working hard. She didn't respond when Jess entered the box but stood with her head hanging down as she had weeks ago.

Jess's confidence in Sonata's future began to flag. She leaned against her, imploring her to get better and gently hugging her. She wondered if there was any point in praying but did so, silently, just in case. Not that it had worked for her father, and when she complained to the rector he had shaken his head sadly, saying that God worked in mysterious ways. I'll say, thought Jess, furiously, but did not say so. It would have been rude and unkind as he was doing his best to comfort her.

"Oh good, she's still on her feet."

Jess spun round, startled nearly out of her wits. Despite the familiarity of the voice her brain took seconds to register that Adam had entered the stable.

"Sorry," he said, grinning.

"Adam!' Jess sounded both cross and relieved. "I nearly died of fright. You're dad said you wouldn't be coming? Is Susan with you?"

"No. I looked in on her and she was flat out and snoring with Marmite alongside. Mum and Dad are watching something noisy on the TV so it was easy to get out."

"But the dogs will bark when you go back, won't they?"

Adam shook his head. "Siani knows my step and Marmite won't hear me from Susan's room."

He let himself into the box and gently stroked Sonata's flank.

"She doesn't seem to be sweating now," Jess said. "She just looks awful."

Adam put a gentle finger on the pulse point above the mare's eye.

"Her pulse is fine. Dad said he was pleased with her quick improvement after giving her an injection. Does Mrs Carey know what's happened?"

"Yes, Mum had to tell her. I'd been really dreading she'd say Sonata would have to be put to sleep, but she said she would rely on Mum's and your dad's judgement. How did you get here?" Jess asked, noticing a striped pyjama top under Adam's anorak.

"Biked. I turned the lights off when I reached your drive. No one saw me. Why isn't there any music on?"

"We stop it about eight or nine." Jess looked at her watch. "Adam, it's nearly eleven! Mum will be taking over soon."

"Crikey, I'd better get back before then. I wonder what she'd say?"

"She'd insist on driving you home but I don't think she'd split on you. What if you're locked out?"

"No hass," said Adam, nonchalantly. "I've three secret ways of getting in that won't trigger the burglar alarm."

Sonata suddenly gave a long, deep sigh.

"She's nearly asleep," said Adam, gently stroking her behind her ears that did not flicker in response. "She's such a sweet old mare. Dad's coming to see her before morning surgery. Don't let on I was here, Jess."

"As if I would," she responded indignantly. "Anyway, I'll have left for school." She gave a sudden shiver. "I'm going to fetch a coat and a drink. Would you like some hot chocolate? I think that's all we've got except for tea or coffee."

Adam said hot chocolate would be fine with two lumps of sugar, and he'd better stay with Sonata in case Pam appeared in the kitchen.

"I'll cough when I come back," said Jess. "If you just hear footsteps you'll know it's Mum and you'll have to hide."

She was back in a few minutes with steaming mugs of chocolate and a packet of biscuits.

"All quiet. I hope Mum oversleeps so I can stay up all night, but I bet she won't."

"Don't they fuss," grumbled Adam. "You'd think we were babies the way they carry on. Still, at least they let us ride when we like and in all weathers."

"Which reminds me, it's just started to rain," said Jess.

Unperturbed, Adam said, "Good thing, specially for our jumping training. When shall we start? Ali and I have orchestra on Thursday, but I s'pose you could make a start with Susan's help."

"Um - I think I'll wait until we're all there. How about Saturday? We could have a hack then school Marmalade."

Adam agreed, glanced at his watch, then drained the last dregs of chocolate. "Better go. Thanks for the choc and biscuits."

Jess accompanied him to the end of the drive. It was raining quite hard and very dark. Adam switched on his lights. They did not shine very far ahead.

"Be careful," warned Jess. "Don't stop for anyone."

Adam burst out laughing. "Now you sound just like the parents."

"Well, there are weirdos about, Adam. It isn't funny."

He rode off, rain spraying from his tyres and Jess ran back to the comfort of the stable.

Remembering her homecoming of twenty-four hours ago, Jess tried to be sensible and prepared for anything as she hurried along the drive. Marmalade and Sonata were not in the paddock; so what did that mean? She dumped her bag and entered the stable to be greeted by whickers coming from adjoining boxes. Overjoyed and weak with relief Jess went first to Sonata, then stopped in her tracks. Protruding from the side of the mare's mouth was a long piece of straw. Gently, Jess pulled it out and dropped it and, at once, the mare's head went down and, daintily, she picked up another piece. Jess looked at her speculatively, then, collecting a head collar from a nearby peg and slipping it over Sonata's head, tied her up on a short rope. Not keen to leave her so restricted for more than a minute, she rushed indoors.

"Mum, she's eating her bed!"

"Who is, darling? Is that your school bag in the yard? I put Marmalade in early as the midges were awful after the rain."

"Oh Mum! Sonata! She's eating straw!"

Her mother stared at her, taking a second to comprehend, then broke into a delighted laugh, hugged Jess, and said, "That could be it!"

"Exactly. She could have given herself colic eating her bed. I must go back, Mum, 'cause I've left her tied up."

Pam hurried after her. Sonata was looking disgruntled. Jess untied her.

"Yes, my lady, I'm afraid you've got to stop that. What can we do, Mum, now I mean? We can't leave her tied in her box until we can change her bedding."

"We'll give her extra food tonight, but first, I'll ring John Barnes. Stay with her, Jess. I'll be very quick."

She was, and returned beaming.

"There's a place just this side of town that sells bales of shredded paper and is open until five-thirty. John thinks we may be right about the colic and, if so, we can be much more confident about her future."

"Oh Mum, that's great! Can we go now? Suppose she eats paper? Wouldn't shavings be safer?"

"I'll go alone so you can keep an eye on Sonata and be here for Mrs Carey. John says paper is better for her breathing than shavings. He says we can increase her food and turn her out much more."

"Of course, she couldn't eat her bed when she was starving because her teeth were so jagged," said Jess.

"That's right. Well, at least we know she has an appetite. I'll dash now, darling, before they close, if you don't mind holding the fort."

Chapter 10

Despite having devoured their Pony Club manuals, and every other instruction book they could lay hands on, the children found their training of Marmalade was unsuccessful.

"We've done it by the book, going over trotting poles, then tiny crossed poles so as not to overface her," complained Susan. "I wonder if it's your fault, Jess, for refusing to hit her."

"I did tap her once," Jess protested, "but she stopped anyway."

Jess was red-faced with exertion and frustration. She had fallen off twice, when Marmalade stopped abruptly, and felt like a beginner. Susan was making matters worse by being critical.

"Mum's called us in for tea," said Adam, scooping Magic from the gatepost and hurrying in.

"Greedy beast," called Susan, then, bossily, to Jess said, "You'd better put Marmalade in the stable; no point in going on if you're going to be so soft with her."

Adam was sitting at the laden table poring over a One Day Event schedule.

"Bradders dropped it in. There's one at home for you, Jess, and I expect there's one for Alison at her gran's."

"Let's see," demanded Susan, leaning across to grab the schedule.

"Don't snatch, yours is on the dresser."

Adam read out the classes for Jess and Alison's benefit.

"There are three sections, minimus, junior, and seniors. It's only six miles from here, at Highbridge Farm. You'll be competing with us, Jess."

"Not if Marmalade won't jump," said Susan nastily, if accurately. "Of course you could go into the minimus section - for practice."

Lin, sensing an atmosphere and having heard Adam's brief account of the problem, suggested, "Why not give Sally a ring? She'll soon sort things out. Go on, Jess, ring her now. You might catch her between lessons."

Jess returned from the hall telephone looking more cheerful.

"She was really nice. She's free after six and willing to help me. Shall we all go along?"

The others nodded.

"Well, that's really good," said Lin. "I'll ring your mum, Jess, and let her know what's happening so she won't worry."

"Gosh thanks," said Jess.

"I'm going to skateboard for a bit, if that's okay, Mum? I've finished my tea."

"Hardly surprising, Adam. You started before everyone else. Yes, on you go."

"So you want to turn Marmalade into a one-day-eventer, but she's not co-operating; right, we must find out why." Sally stood, hands on hips, looking at Jess and Marmalade, watched by Susan, Adam and Alison.

"There's no reason why a well-schooled and balanced pony shouldn't jump happily, particularly if it's never been forced or frightened.. Obviously, that hasn't happened to Marmalade as she loves cross-country jumping. Right, let's go into the school and warm her up a bit."

While Jess did as Sally suggested, the others arranged trotting poles and a tiny jump of crossed poles.

"That's exactly what we did at home, and she refused," said Susan critically.

"Her refusing may have had nothing to do with the course," said Sally. "Now go over the poles a few times, Jess, then go on round to the little jump, keeping her very straight and using your legs strongly."

The trotting poles were no longer a problem; Marmalade went over them without faltering. She trotted calmly towards the jump and reaching it stopped dead. Jess made her step over it to cries of, "Good girl, keep her moving," from Sally. "Now walk deliberately over the jump a couple of times as if that's what you always wanted her to do; then try trotting again."

Jess did as Sally instructed. Again Marmalade stopped from trot but Jess made her walk over the little jump.

"Should I hit her?" called Jess, exasperated.

"No. I've nothing against tapping a pony if it's being awkward but I don't think that's the case with Marmalade. Let's go out to the field where I've some natural-looking fences."

They all followed Sally past the indoor school into the field alongside it.

"There's a little ditch, then a cut-and-laid hedge leading into a paddock, and you come back over a log pile. That's my apology for a cross-country course having always used Lord Connor's. Now try to forget about us and ride off and enjoy yourself. Pretend you're on Exmoor."

Jess grinned thinking how difficult that would be! She squeezed Marmalade on into a smooth canter and they flew the ditch in fine style. Steadying Marmalade who was now clearly enjoying herself, Jess continued towards the little hedge.

"Oh brilliant!" called Sally and the others, as pony and rider disappeared into the paddock. They hurried towards the log pile to watch their return jump which was faultless.

"Good. Make a big fuss of her. Now we'll return to the show jumps."
Jess groaned but led the way.

"I still think you should hit her when she refuses," said Susan, bossily.

Adam looked embarrassed for her and wished she'd keep quiet. Sally just smiled.

"What would Tara do if you hit her - really HIT her, I mean?"

Susan went slightly pink and replied, "Um - I think she'd go berserk."

"Yes, I think she would. Marmalade would react differently and would probably end up soured. Of course, a little tap is sometime necessary to get the pony's attention or to curtail a bad habit, but if I had my way whips would be banned for punishment."

"I'd hate to hit Pie," said Adam, seizing a rare chance to score over Susan.

"You never would. You'd be more likely to hit Susan," said Alison.

"I can't imagine you'd need to hit Pie." Sally grinned. "I'm not so sure about Susan. Now, Jess, will you hop off for a minute?"

Jess dismounted and slipped Marmalade a polo mint.

"Really," Sally continued, "you've all done well. There's nothing wrong with the way you've been training Marmalade. The problem is with the rider." Sally paused to let her words sink in. All the children felt slightly uncomfortable, Adam, Susan and Alison on Jess's behalf.

"I'm not criticising your riding, Jess; generally, it's very good but did you pick up jumping as part of your normal rides?"

Surprised, Jess nodded. Her lessons with her mother had ended when her father became very ill; so she and Marmalade had learnt to jump together on the moor.

Sally turned to the others, asking, "Was there anything different about Jess's style in the field, compared with how she rode here?"

They all looked at one another for inspiration, then Alison said, "They looked happy in the field."

"Excellent. They were happy and relaxed. How do you look if you're not happy on a pony?"

"Tense."

"Right."

"Oh good one, Susan," muttered Adam.

Ignoring him Sally continued: "You were really going with your pony in the field but here you were simply sitting on her. Your tension made you perch. Anything else you noticed?"

"Jess leaned forward much more in the school," volunteered Alison.

"Yes. You anticipated the jump and by the time you arrived at it your weight was too far forward. Marmalade felt it was all wrong so she stopped, like the sensible native pony she is."

Sally scratched Marmalade's poll and received a gentle nudge by way of approval. She chuckled and dug into her pocket for a couple of pony nuts.

"May I ride her for a few minutes?"

"Yes, of course." Jess let down the stirrups.

Sally checked the strap of her hard hat and Marmalade's girth, then mounted lightly. Apart from her legs being a bit long she didn't look too big. She squeezed Marmalade into walk, then trotted to pick up the pony's rhythm and, finally, urged her to canter.

"She's beautifully responsive," she enthused, then, to the surprise of the watching children, rode towards a jump made of two brightly coloured planks. Marmalade soared over it. The children cheered and clapped. Next, Sally rode towards the crossed poles which the pony flew. Twice more Sally rode over the two little jumps, then she dismounted and made a great fuss of Marmalade, joined by the delighted children.

"D'you mind being a guinea pig again, Jess?" asked Sally, shortening the stirrups. "We're all learning with you."

"Gosh no," exclaimed Jess, thinking how different Sally's teaching was from Mrs Trotman's. She was sure Sally would have spotted the problem if she'd been taking that awful rally. She mounted and checked her stirrups.

"Start with the crossed poles and keep your bottom firmly on the saddle. Fold from the hips just before the take-off. Practice it now - yes, that's it! Now, when you're ready..."

But Jess was off, riding a circle then cantering slowly towards the first jump. It looked as if it was going to be all right, but Jess panicked and leaned forward too soon, so Marmalade stopped.

"Don't worry. You won't crack it in a couple of minutes. This time I'll shout `now`; so don't fold until I tell you."

It worked. Jess resisted the strong impulse to lean forward, got very slightly left behind but did not jab Marmalade's mouth and they sailed over. With everyone cheering, Jess rode to the next jump.

"You've cracked it," yelled Adam as they flew over the planks.

"Just one more," called Sally, but Jess did not hear and they flew over the poles and the planks again.

Laughing, Sally walked to meet her. "Very well done. Keep this up and you'll be fine. D'you remember singing nursery rhymes at your early rallies?"

Jess shook her head. "I'm a very new member."

Sally looked surprised. "Well, the others will remember. We often encourage the younger ones to sing as they ride down a grid - a line of tiny jumps, usually poles. It helps the riders to relax; so if you find yourself tensing up take some deep breaths and sing something easy; *Baa... baa... black sheep* is a favourite."

Jess laughed and hugged Marmalade. "Sally, I've lots of pocket money saved up; there was nowhere to spend it at home - only I haven't any on me now."

"Jess, there's nothing to pay. It was a pleasure to help you. After all, you helped me - you and Alison - when Mackie died."

Jess swallowed hard. "That's really kind, Sally. I... I'm so sorry about Mackie."

Sally smiled sadly, shaking her head. "It's impossible to understand... How could anyone…"

Her voice tailed off as the others joined them. In seconds they had booked a group dressage lesson with no words of dissent from Susan. Alison said that as the average camel could do a better dressage test than Linus it should be very amusing for the other ponies.

"But not for you riders," said Sally laughing. "I shall expect very best efforts."

They all thanked Sally then, and set off for home on bikes and pony.

"I'm going to have to practice such a lot for the one day event," said Jess, now more determined than apprehensive.

"Same here," said Alison, "but Adam and I have to practice for the end of term concert too."

"So you may have to manage without us," said Adam, grinning. "It'll be tough for you..."

"Big head," said Susan, swerving perilously near his bike.

"Sally says I can show one of her small hunters during the holidays; so I've got to learn how to use double reins," said Alison.

"Gosh, you lucky duck," exclaimed Susan, not without a touch of envy.

"Well - yes I am - but I haven't got my own pony, and that's what I'd like more than anything."

"Is it absolutely impossible?" asked Jess.

"Yes. When Dad left he took all our money. That's why Mum has to work so hard 'cause we've had to start again from scratch."

Jess looked so horrified that Alison giggled.

"Oh, it's not too bad. Granny's been brilliant to us although she's Dad's mother. She's very cross with him."

At the twin's turning Alison volunteered to continue with Jess as she had lights on her bike.

"Thanks, but won't you be late home?"

Alison grinned. "I don't want to be early. Gran's got the Church fête meeting at home. They're all okay only they seem to think I'm about six. And they think I'm missing Dad but coming to live here has been great, and Mum comes home most weekends."

Marmalade trotted along beside Alison's bike seeming to enjoy the quiet swishing of the tyres.

"I think they find bikes soothing," Alison said, "but Marmalade is brilliant with all sorts of traffic. How did that happen when Exmoor is so remote – not like the New Forest."

"We sent her to a friend near Porlock with a field bordering the coast road. She saw every kind of traffic you could imagine," Jess explained.

"Like in Black Beauty, only in her case it was trains. D'you know, Jess, I don't think I'll ever be able to read that chapter called `Poor Ginger' again. It's the saddest thing I've ever read."

"Same here," Jess agreed. "I know it had to be written like that to really shock people into doing something for cab horses, but it's really horrible."

"Adam once told me he read `Tarka the Otter' when he was really little and didn't realise Tarka dies." Alison said. "He read it again last year and was really upset."

Alison's bike wobbled as Marmalade slowed to a walk and she put a hand on the pony's neck to steady herself. They rode in companionable silence for a while, breathing in the mingled scents that make a summer evening so special.

"I s'pose you live in Tarka country," Alison said suddenly. "Have you seen an otter?"

"Only once. We're a few miles from Tarka's area but Daddy and I spent days and days there looking for otters one summer. Eventually, we saw one basking by the roots of a tree. We were quiet as mice watching from the other bank but it quickly sensed we were there and slid into the river completely disappearing."

"You are lucky. It must have been wonderful."

"It was. Well - the next most wonderful thing after Mary and Marmalade's rescue from the blizzard."

"Gosh, yes it would be hard to beat that. I s'pose the farmer gave them to you out of gratitude."

Jess gave a hoot of laughter. "Gosh no, he wasn't like that. We paid for Marmalade but he said we could hardly have one without the other and Contrary Mary was more trouble than she was worth to him. Perhaps he did feel a bit guilty. He did know Mary was missing because Mum rang him to ask if she'd moved down near his farm with the rest of the herd. He said he hadn't bothered to check as he was pretty sure she wasn't in foal. She'd been barren for two years."

"So he really didn't care?"

"That's right. Mum said she'd give him time to check and would ring him back in half-an-hour but by then the 'phone lines had collapsed with the weight of snow. Obviously, Mum couldn't chance that Mary had been found so she and Daddy went to the place they'd last seen her, about three days before. Granny and I were afraid they'd get lost so we put oil lamps in all the windows and Mum said they could see them all the time although it was snowing. We didn't get electricity or the 'phone back for five days. Mum's great dread was that we'd need the vet, but luckily we didn't."

"How long did Mary live?"

"Nearly three years. She died in her sleep under her favourite hawthorn tree."

"Did Marmalade miss her dreadfully?"

"No. Well, not noticeably. She really does seem to be as happy with people as with ponies."

Alison chuckled and smoothed her hand along the pony's mane. "Here's your drive. I'll go back now. I expect the old ducks' have gone home."

"Thanks for coming with me. See you tomorrow. You're borrowing Linus, aren't you?"

"Yes. Bye."

As Jess led Marmalade into the stable loud whinnying greeted them, a sure sign of Sonata's recovery. Jess went to-and-fro mixing feeds, and filling hay nets, and all the while talking to Sonata who watched every move from her door.

Outside, filling the water buckets, Jess looked west at the brilliant pink-tinged sky. Soon the first star would appear; was it Venus? It always looked really close to the moon. Poor Marmalade confined to the stable and missing all this!

Since Mackie's death there had been no more attacks. The letter had provoked horse lovers to demand action from the police and there had been many replies. Had the killer been frightened off? Had he gone to ground never to be caught? One thing was certain, there was no indication that horse owners could relax their vigilance.

After replacing the buckets, Jess cleaned the grease from her tack with a damp sponge. The sound of footsteps outside caught her attention and for a second she froze, then her mother's voice called: "Jess – oh, you are back safely."

She relaxed. "Yes, have you been worried?"

"Not really. Lin kindly rang to tell me what you were doing, but it's nice to see you."

She came in and stroked Sonata's nose. Marmalade glanced round and whickered then returned to her hay net. Jess noticed her blue dress and loose hair, almost reaching her shoulders. A pleasant change from the neat bun that went with her efficient nurse's image.

"Hours go by and I don't see you," Pam said, wistfully.

"You're always busy with Mrs Carey," Jess replied, a shade peevishly.

"Well, now we are together tell me how you got on."

So Jess gave her a detailed account of her day, while tidying up and carefully locking the stable door.

In the kitchen Pam picked up a thick cloth and bent to open the bottom oven. "I've kept your supper hot - Cassoulet."

She put an earthenware pot on the table and lifted the lid.

"Hmm, smells good. Did Maggie make it?"

"No, I did."

"Thanks, Mum, I'm starving. Have you eaten?"

"Yes, I ate early with Mrs Carey. She's had an eventful day too. She used the lift for the first time and it works perfectly. She so wanted you to be there but she had me, Jenny and Maggie as an enthralled audience. Would you go up to see her when you've finished your supper? She's longing to tell you all about it."

Jess sighed. She was half way through an exciting book and wanted to read in bed.

"Oh... I s'pose so." She helped herself to vegetables.

"You know, Jess, she really likes you. I know she slightly resented you at first..."

"Slightly! Come of it, Mum, she wanted to pack me off to boarding school."

"Darling, you're exaggerating; anyway that was weeks ago, it never comes up now."

"No, of course not, now I'm her groom."

Instantly Jess regretted her words. She loved looking after Sonata and would have hated it if a proper groom had been engaged.

"Jess, the past weeks can't have been easy for you, and I really feel proud of the way you've coped. Our way of life has changed so much, and mine is changing again. Now Mrs Carey can get out I'm to be her driver as well as her nurse. A mechanic is coming to overhaul her Rover next week."

"I s'pose our old car isn't good enough."

"Oh yes it is, but in my opinion it's far too uncomfortable for a severely arthritic old lady. However, she is going in it tomorrow to visit Sam. She's so excited."

"So I'll see even less of you, Mum, if you're going to start gadding about."

"Not necessarily, darling, you could come gadding with us."

"No thanks. Anyway, we're all riding tomorrow."

Pam opened the fridge and took out a glass bowl. "Lemon mousse, one of your favourites."

"Thanks."

Jess ate silently, wishing she didn't feel so horrid. She'd had a really good day and now it was if a black cloud had descended on her to spoil it.

Pam set up the ironing board and began sorting out a basket of dry clothes while Jess carried dishes to the sink and ran hot water into the bowl. She bent to switch on the electric iron for Pam.

"Don't touch a switch with wet hands, please Jess – ever. It's so dangerous."

"Sorry." She washed up wishing she could go straight to bed. Then Alison's words came into her mind and kept repeating themselves: 'Mum comes home *most* weekends' and 'When Dad left he took all our money'. Suddenly, she put down the tea towel and gave her mother a hug.

"Sorry, Mum. I know I'm really horrid sometimes but I don't mean it."

"I know. Even Daddy and I were horrid to each other at times, but we still loved each other. I'll go up to Mrs Carey and tell her you'll see her in the morning. You look very tired."

"No, I will go up, Mum, just for five minutes. And now Sonata seems to be getting better, I'd like to visit Sam - not tomorrow but quite soon."

"He'll be so pleased." Pam beamed. "He's longing for first-hand news of Sonata."

"Gosh, Mum, I'll have to be very careful what I say. I mean, he thinks she's always been in wonderful condition!"

Laughing, Pam said, "One thing is sure, he must never know how she really was."

Chapter 11

A month later Pam was leaning on the gate enjoying rare idleness while Jess trundled a lightweight barrow around the paddock shovelling up droppings. After a hot day the air was heady with the scent of roses, lavender, honeysuckle and newly mown grass. Swallows swooped between the stable loft and the telephone cable, their backs fired by the evening sun. Maggie had told Jess to be sure to leave the louvres open for their homecoming and, in May, she'd counted five nests in the loft.

Marmalade and Sonata followed Jess, swishing their tails against midges.

"Best time to put them out would be about ten," Jess said regretfully, "and keep them in during the day."

"Yes, but they'd eat all night and get too fat. At least they're forced to stand under the trees for several hours in the day. I always renew their fly stuff at lunchtime; so they don't have too bad a time."

"Mum, you're a saint. You wouldn't like to clean the paddocks?"

"No thanks. How did yesterday's dressage practice go?"

"Pretty well. It's certainly easier in a proper arena and we all had room to work together. Sally helped us after she finished work."

"How is Linus doing?"

"Really well. He looks heaps better and is much more obedient. He and Alison seem to suit each other."

"Do tell Mrs Carey all about it."

"She's at the window," Jess said, waving. "Mum, her sight seems to have improved suddenly."

"It has. We went to an optician a couple of weeks ago, and she was able to help her a bit. She'd been wearing the same spectacles for twenty years. She asked me to go up to the attic this morning to inspect Sonata's tack. It's in wonderful condition, well oiled, even wrapped in oily cloths. There's a sidesaddle and two bridles. Mrs Carey rode astride, except at shows, but gave that saddle away years ago. I feel slightly anxious that she's been circling advertisements for synthetic, lightweight saddles in Horse and Hound."

"Oh Mum, she's not thinking of riding, surely?"

"No." Pam chuckled. "I think she has ambitions for me - or you. She's renting the `Highlights of Badminton' video on Saturday and wants us and Ali and the twins to have supper and watch it with her."

"Oh Mum, sometimes she's lovely. I know Ali and the twins will want to."

Above them a window opened and Mrs Carey called, "Why not try riding Sonata around the paddock?"

Jess looked inquiringly at Pam, who grinned.

"All right, I'll get the head collar and your hat while you empty the barrow."

Minutes late, Sonata stood like a rock while Pam gave Jess a leg up.

"Ouch, it's a bit like sitting on a knife edge." Jess grimaced. "And terrifically high up."

Pam laughed and squinted up at her. "You look a bit distant. Shall I lead her on?"

"No thanks, just hold the end of the rope. I want to see how responsive she is just to my legs."

At a gentle squeeze Sonata walked on quietly, accompanied by Pam and then Marmalade who nudged her in the rear.

"She doesn't need help, Marmalade," Pam reproved.

"Gosh Mum, she's incredible," exclaimed Jess, and indeed she was. At the lightest touch she moved forward, sideways, halted and even lengthened her stride.

"She must have been a dream to ride." Jess beamed up at Mrs Carey who clapped with delight, as excited as a child.

"Sometime, try her in a bridle," she called.

After a few minutes Jess dismounted, landing with a jolt, not having prepared herself for the distance. Marmalade gave her a nudge but whether of sympathy or reproach they could not tell; so Jess gave her a consoling Polo Mint.

The following day Jess worked hard, trying to learn a dressage test, with Pam's help.

"A. Enter at working trot. X. Walk. G. Halt. Salute, proceed at medium walk. C. track right, M.B.F. working trot, rising.... I can do all that with my eyes shut, it's the rest I can't remember."

Pam smiled sympathetically. "You'll be fine on the day. I used to feel exactly like you and yet it all seemed to fall into place as I rode up the centre line."

Unconvinced, Jess said, "I know I could have it read, but that is a bit feeble unless there's a really good reason. Susan says one of our prefects, in another branch, always has his tests read, but he's dyslexic."

"Oh, I think I met his mother at a W.I. meeting I went to with Jenny. He's brilliant at science."

"Well, I'm not brilliant at anything, not even learning a dressage test."

"Maybe you're trying too hard. Haven't you rather overdone the dressage lately?"

"Only 'cause it's been too hard to jump, and I don't think we've made the ponies stale."

"No, I was thinking of you becoming stale. Why don't you go for a walk. It's so lovely out now. I'd come but I'm taking Mrs Carey to Evensong."

"Oh - perhaps. I wish the others were around."

"Jess, they'll all be back on Tuesday and have only been away since Friday when you broke up. You used to be really happy on your own."

"I still am, Mum, but not all the time. It's a bit much all of them going away before the One Day Event."

"That's on Saturday. You'll have time together for a last practice. Now, I really must go and change."

Jess watched her mother's disappearing back, sighed and stretched, tipping her chair precariously backwards. Perhaps her mother was right about being a bit stale. Maybe a ride would make her feel better.

She put fly repellent around Marmalade's eyes and ears, then ran the sponge down her legs and under her belly. There were already midges about so, impulsively, she rubbed the sponge over her bare arms. At once she realised what a silly thing she had done and went indoors to wash. Pam always warned her to read instructions and use such products correctly. Still, she felt all right and not as if she were about to keel over. As she reached the lobby the telephone rang in the kitchen.

"Bother," she said, wanting to ignore it but, perhaps, it was important.

"Hello Jess, it's Sally. You know I'm on the Pony Club committee, well, we've all been asked by Mrs Bradshaw to ring round to local members and spread the news, which isn't very good."

"Oh gosh, whatever is it? Has the One Day Event been cancelled?"

"No, although the ground is harder than we'd have liked but sawdust will be put down. In a way it's more disappointing; it's about Lord Connor's woods - they're now out-of-bounds."

"Oh no, so we've lost the argument?"

"For the present, but we've lots of people on our side, and Alison's mother is giving us free legal advice. I'm afraid we'll have to obey the new owner's instructions meanwhile. Could you let the others know? You'll probably see them before I do, except Ali, maybe."

"Yes, of course. Thanks for ringing, Sally. See you on Saturday."

"D'you want to stable Marmalade here for the night, or will you hack down in the morning?"

"I'll hack down, thanks. What time will you load up?"

"Oh, about eight-fifteen. Marmalade can be last in. She boxes well, doesn't she?"

"Yes, loves it, only she'd rather be in the cab."

Sally laughed and rang off and, for a minute, Jess stood beside the telephone feeling disappointed and cross. Some of their best rides had been in the woods. She switched on the burglar alarm just inside the back door, locked up and hid the key.

"We should have ridden in the woods as often as possible instead of doing all this dressage," she grumbled to Marmalade who nudged her in agreement. "Dressage is all very well but there isn't a lot of excitement in it."

Slowly tightening the girth, she continued, "The woods are always moist and springy underfoot. Well, we'll jolly well go there now, probably for the last time."

Her irritation gone after riding a while, Jess gave a huge sigh of relief when she arrived at the hunting gate and saw it was unlocked. Well, if the new Lord Connor was keen to keep riders out of the wood, he should have done something to prevent them getting in!

Marmalade stepped out eagerly, anticipating some fun. They followed the route Jess had been introduced to weeks ago; the logs, then the low, fixed pole followed by the brush fence. Marmalade flew them all keenly but not rushing. Jess patted her and brought her back to trot for a few yards, then squeezed her on to a brisk, but controlled, canter to take the middle height of the next three jumps. As it was pleasantly cool and the going was good, Jess decided to take the long circuit that went to the edge of the wood. Following an incline, she glimpsed sheep in an adjoining field and many rabbits playing and eating. Remembering Adam's accident, she was watchful for deer, but guessed they had probably left the wood to graze in local fields in the coolness of evening.

There was one jump she very much wanted to try, more for herself than Marmalade. It was a wide bank shored up with railway sleepers; so one had to jump onto it deliberately and carefully and, jumping from either direction, there was quite a drop on landing. Sensibly, Jess rode the lowest option but, even so, had difficulty going with her pony on take-off, and helped herself by clutching a handful of mane.

"Good girl," she enthused, patting Marmalade, and was quite pleased with her own performance as she had managed to slip the reins on landing.

She was relieved to see Marmalade wasn't sweating. Further along this ride was a low wall, topped with a pole that they had jumped only once. Patting Marmalade enthusiastically for clearing it with a foot to spare, she said, "Clever, clever girl. We'll go back through the stream - you'll love that - then we'll head for home."

She glanced at her watch but it wasn't on her wrist, and she remembered removing it to scrub her arms. "Bother, we've probably another hour but I can't be sure. Maybe just a one or two more jumps, before the stream."

Squinting up through the trees it was hard to judge the lightness of the sky, but there was still plenty of birdsong, and with Marmalade going so well and happily it was too tempting not to take small jumps, do controlled trotting, and then walk on a long rein. At the stream Marmalade splashed in and lowered her head to drink. Jess allowed her a mouthful, then they walked on at a leisurely pace to join the main ride.

Jess thought about the events of the past weeks. The dressage training sessions and a time at Laburnum Lodge when they had a pretend competition under B.S.J.A. rules. Relying on the large second-hand on his alarm clock to time a jump-off, Adam had accidentally touched the wrong button. Leaping a foot into the air, their nerves shattered by the clanging, Tara and Marmalade had dumped their riders on the ground. Too weak with laughter to continue Susan and Jess agreed to divide the first prize - a double Mars bar. Then the ground became too hard for jumping and for two weeks they had concentrated on dressage.

Jess had kept her promise to visit Sam in hospital. They'd talked nineteen-to-the-dozen while Pam and Jenny, Sam's daughter, delighted they were getting on so well, spent time with a patient who never had visitors.

Marmalade's hooves were silent on the peaty floor of the wood. She stretched into the loose rein, and sensing they were homeward bound, lengthened her stride in a way that does not come easily to Exmoor ponies.

Berrywood gate was close. Jess glanced upwards and saw just a snippet of yellowing sky. The birds had gone quiet giving only an occasional call. Oh dear, it was later than she thought. She shivered. There were goose pimples on her bare arms. It had grown strangely cold. A rasping sound caught her attention. It was not a natural noise made by a bird or animal, but the kind that sets the teeth on edge, like chalk scratching on a blackboard.

They rounded a bend; abruptly Marmalade stopped, head raised, ears sharply pricked. Following the line of her gaze Jess saw a tall figure leaning against a tree not thirty feet away. It was a swarthy-looking, longhaired youth in dark clothes, absorbed in drawing a very long, thin knife across a wet stone. In the same line of vision, beyond him, under the fringe of trees was a splash of green meadow and there, placidly grazing, were a mare and foal.

The instant Jess knew she was looking at the horse attacker, he turned and saw them. He gave a violent start, stared for a second with a look of vicious fury, then lunged forward. For a second Jess froze like a mesmerised rabbit, then, as if pony and rider shared a primitive instinct for survival beyond conscious thought, Jess's right leg moved a fraction and Marmalade spun into a half pirouette. There was a flash of steel and a jerk on the left rein but nothing impeded Marmalade's leap into a headlong gallop along the way they had come.

Crouching over the withers like a jockey Jess had never ridden so fast. Her pony's flying hooves showered the air with clods of earth. Dimly she was aware of passing familiar landmarks, a log pile, low hurdles and the bullfinch. They bypassed the jumps without slackening speed but soon the denseness of the wood forced them to slow down. Looking around Jess realised she now didn't know where she was. She must have crossed the main track, galloping blindly in any direction that was away from danger. They hadn't crossed the stream; so she reckoned they had ridden a diagonal line towards the far right-hand corner.

The only sounds she could hear were her painfully thudding heart and her breath coming out in great rasping sobs. Perhaps she could be heard all over the wood? Marmalade's hoof prints must be all too noticeable. She glanced over her shoulder, fearful that she would see a dark figure slipping through the trees. They had to keep moving and, trotting in and out as if in a bending race, she prayed Marmalade would not trip over a bramble cable or put her foot down a hole.

Many of the trees were marked for felling and much of the undergrowth had been cleared. Soon they came to the boundary fence and followed it leftwards. Jess was looking for the only other gate she knew. At the far end of the main track it let onto a gravel drive that eventually joined a lane running into Berrywood village. Only once had she ridden this route coming from the other direction. She remembered riding past a keeper's cottage and the twins waving to a woman working in the garden.

The trees were thinning and suddenly there was the main track and a five bar gate. Jess turned sharp right, again looking behind her but there was no one in sight. Beyond the gate a drive curved away through the trees but there was no cottage. It had to be further on.

She ran her hand along Marmalade's neck and shoulder. She was hardly sweating and showing no sign of distress. Jess hugged her and whispered that she was the best pony in the world. She didn't want to dismount; Marmalade was her rescuer, her security but, she remembered, it hadn't been possible to open the heavy gate from horseback. The three girls had ragged Adam for his gallantry in jumping off Pie and hauling the gate open. But, scarlet-faced, he'd protested that it wasn't gallantry; just that they were so feeble he'd got on with it.

About to pull the stiff lever she wailed aloud; the gate was locked with a stout chain and padlock. She gave a futile tug, looking around frantically for some other way. Marmalade gently nudged her elbow as if to say, 'Come on, we can't stay here all night.' And soon it would be night! Hugging her pony for comfort she scanned the fence. No hope there! Very taut sheep wire, topped with several strands of barbed wire stretched away on either side. Yet she only had to climb over the gate and run for safety, but what of her beloved pony? To leave her alone was unthinkable. Then into her mind flashed an idea. Mentally, she measured Marmalade's height against the gate. A more daring feat of riding than she had ever undertaken seemed the only way. She remounted, trotted twenty yards from the gate then turned quietly to face it.

"Please God, help us to do it," she said aloud, and pretending with every scrap of her imagination that she was about to win Badminton, cantered towards the final obstacle.

"You can do it, Marmalade!" she cried, trying desperately to ride with all her heart and strength. She shut her eyes as the pony soared into the air. They seemed to be suspended for ages, then a jolt told her they had landed. She opened her eyes and glanced back at the receding gate.

"Brilliant pony, you're brilliant," she cried, tears of relief streaming down her cheeks.

Around the bend was a stand of ash trees and the cottage with a telephone cable running to its roof. She wanted to shout and cheer with joy but drew up quietly at the gate and dismounted, feeling as wobbly as if she had been on the most terrifying ride in a fairground. She looped the reins over the gatepost, told Marmalade to stand, and then walked unsteadily to the door. She gave three loud raps with the brass knocker shaped like a dog's head and stood, anxiously waiting, under an arched trellis covered with purple clematis. She heard a distant bark and was about to knock again when she heard the scrunch of footsteps on gravel. A tall bearded man came round the side of the house. He smiled amiably.

"Water for you or for the pony? 'Tis usually one or t'other."

"No thanks..." Jess took a deep breath. "It's the horse killer - he's in the woods - near the mare and foal."

The man had kind eyes and a friendly face but, as Jess's words sank in and he saw her distress, his expression changed. She wouldn't want to be a poacher caught with one of his pheasants! He put a hand on her shoulder and patted her as he would his dog, calling over his shoulder, "Lydia... Lyd... Come on out here a minute."

He unlatched the gate and gently led Marmalade inside.

"Will she stand here quietly?"

"Yes," Jess ran the stirrups up, and the keeper put the reins behind them then Jess slackened the girth.

"Nice pony... Exmoor?"

"Yes," Jess smiled for the first time, then, remembering a mare and foal were in grave danger if not already dead, cried, "It's terribly urgent. He had a knife - was sharpening it when I saw him. He tried - to grab M - Marmalade..." Her voice went out of control.

The keeper's wife was beside her, putting an arm around her shoulders. At the sight of her fair hair tied back the way Pam sometimes wore hers and her kind face full of concern, Jess burst into tears.

Chapter 12

The keeper was ringing the police station and grumbling about the time it was taking. Jess sat in an armchair beside the Rayburn that was obviously alight as a huge black kettle was hissing on the hob. Gosh, it was hot! No wonder geraniums bloomed in profusion on the windowsills. A spaniel rested its muzzle on Jess's knee, looking at her soulfully. She fondled its ears.

"Alf, it's Bill Selwood; nasty business near Berrywood gate. Young lady rider came across a bloke with a knife... Yes, seemed to be watching our mare and foal... Oh, yes he saw her all right; would've attacked her if she hadn't galloped off. No, she's not hurt... Right... About ten minutes ago, maybe longer... Great. See you then."

Bill smiled briefly at Jess then, while dialling another number, said, "There is a patrol car on its way now. Luckily there was one not half a mile away. They're going straight to the field."

Jess gratefully accepted a cup of tea from Lydia who had disappeared for a few minutes.

"Ronnie, get a trailer down to Gemma and her foal quick as you can... Yes, go straight across the fields, it's bone dry."

Jess heard Bill repeat her story to Lord Connor's groom. He looked very upset when he put the receiver down.

"Gem's the last horse bred by his late Lordship, and Sapphire's her first foal. I'm meeting Ronnie down there, Lyd."

He reached for his gun and a key hanging on a hook behind the scullery door. He stared at the key for a second, then looked at Jess with incredulity. "How did you get out of the wood? The agent had the gates locked yesterday."

She grinned. "Not the Berrywood gate. He forgot that one. And we jumped over the other one to get out."

Bill gave a low whistle to express his admiration, and Lydia said, "You could have been killed!"

"Could have if she'd stayed in the wood," said Bill, grimly. "Your nearside rein is slashed nearly through."

"Gosh, I didn't know. Must've happened when he tried to grab me."

Bill walked outside shaking his head in amazed admiration. Lydia poured second cups of tea and started cutting bread for sandwiches while Jess telephoned The Elms but there was no reply.

"They can't be back from Church," she explained to Lydia. "If I'm not back when it's dark Mum will be really worried."

"We'll keep trying. Now you eat something, lovey. Keep up with your pony."

"Oh, I must check Marmalade. She must be worried."

"You sit tight and rest," advised Lydia. "She's had a drink, half a pound of carrots and I've put an old quilt over her in case she breaks out in a sweat."

"Gosh, that's really kind." Jess beamed at her.

"I'm no rider. Certainly not like you but we've always had horses on the estate, so I've picked up a bit about looking after them."

There was the sound of car wheels on the gravel and, minutes later, a policewoman and a younger policeman were tucking into tea and sandwiches while listening to Jess's story.

Gosh, they were making her work hard! How tall was the man? What sort of build? What was he wearing? Did he speak? Jess struggled to remember accurately but it had all happened so fast. Suddenly, a picture flashed into her mind.

"I could draw him," she said. "I'm sure I could draw him better than I'm describing him."

At once Lydia found paper in Bill's desk and a jar full of pencils. Jess's task now became easy. Not watching her or talking, the police officers gratefully accepted more tea and the younger one made a fuss of Delilah, the spaniel who was heavily in whelp.

"There, hope that's all right," said Jess, handing the drawing to the woman officer.

Absolutely silent for half a minute the officers stared at the drawing, then at each other, and finally at Jess. Their faces wore huge, satisfied grins.

"Our prime suspect. It could be a photograph."

"You mean you really recognise him?"

"Yes, Jess, we certainly do! Now, can we put the rest of the story together? How did you escape?"

When Jess reached the bit about jumping the gate, both officers sat open-mouthed staring at her. At last the policeman recovered his powers of speech.

"This – er - Marmalade, what sort of horse is he?"

"*She*..." Lydia forestalled Jess. "A small native pony, an Exmoor. They were both brilliant."

"Whew." The man was goggle-eyed.

Jess blushed and tried to look matter-of-fact. She wanted to giggle as she had a fleeting picture in her mind of a winged Pegasus, in the shape of her chunky Exmoor mare, flying high above a Panda car. She would have to draw it later.

"Excuse me," said Lydia, "but we must try ringing Jess's mother again. Lovey, shall I talk to her first. Assure her you're okay?"

Jess nodded gratefully and minutes later talked to Pam who was very concerned but calm.

"I'll come and collect you, but what about Marmalade?"

Jess asked Lydia who assured her Marmalade would be taken home in a trailer, and then the sergeant said Jess would be driven home shortly. She had a few words with Pam, saying how helpful Jess had been, and then she rang the station.

"I want to get his lodging watched. He may even be there already. They're on their way? Good work."

She turned to Jess, beaming but, before she could speak, Bill came charging in, crying,

"Both are safe!"

There were hugs all round then Bill described what had happened. There had been an attack. The mare was very nervous, lashing out at everyone except Ronnie. Once in the trailer she had calmed down and they were able to examine her and the foal.

"Any injuries?" asked Lydia, anxiously.

"Not to Gemma, but the foal was cut behind the off-side ear."

"Badly?"

"She'll need stitches but she's not in danger."

"Oh, will Mr Barnes do that?" Jess asked, keen for him to be part of the adventure.

"No, we've used the Manston practice for years. "

"What about the killer, was he caught?"

"The police are still searching but there's not a lot of hope of finding him in the area now."

"Luckily we have this marvellous drawing made by Jess," said Sergeant Pollard. "We've had our eye on him since the attack at Berrywood stables." She handed the paper to Bill.

"Then why haven't you arrested him?" asked Jess, challengingly.

"We didn't have enough to go on but thanks to you we certainly have now. As soon as he turns up at his lodgings we'll nab him."

"D'you know this young lady is not only an artist, she's a crack rider," Bill told the police officers.

"Oh we realise that," said Sergeant Pollard. "Jess is the heroine this evening."

"Ronnie thinks so," said Bill, handing the drawing back. "He's bringing the trailer back for Marmalade."

"Won't he want to stay with the foal?" Jess asked.

"He's got an assistant who'll stay. Truth is, he wants to meet you so he can say his thanks, and give a proper account to the new guv'nor. Thinks it'll give him plenty to think about. No, Jess, if you wanted to go to John

O'Groats tonight Ronnie'd drive you!"

And so Jess and Marmalade travelled home in the wake of the police car. Had everyone not still been up, the relieved and affectionate whinnying would certainly have woken them. Anxious to get back to his horses Ronnie declined Pam's offer of a drink, but the two police officers stayed for ten minutes talking to Pam and Mrs Carey.

Astonished to see the old lady up and dressed so late, Jess registered that she had known the policeman all his life. Once he had even been caught scrumping in her orchard.

"Frightened the life out of me did the Colonel, then I had a hiding when I got home. Still, I never pinched anything again," he told them, grinning at this surprising recollection. "Good man, the Colonel and I remember you on your lovely horses, Mrs Carey."

Beaming, she said, "Thanks to Jess I still have my last one."

Jess couldn't stay to hear the familiar story; almost asleep on her feet, she just managed to make polite farewells before being gently led off to bed by Pam.

The heat from a shaft of sunlight crossing her arm awoke her. To let some air in the curtains were not fully drawn across the open window and, drowsily, she assessed by the brightness of the room that it was mid-morning.

Dash, still no watch! She must retrieve it from the downstairs cloakroom. She sat up, yawning widely and stretching her arms above her head. It was half a minute before she had sorted out why she was sleeping so late, not at school, and still feeling tired!

From the landing her mother calling quietly, "Are you awake?"

"Yes - just."

Pam came in carrying a tray that she put on a stool beside the bed. "Tea and there's muesli and fruit, and honey toast."

"Wow - breakfast in bed. It isn't Christmas, is it?"

Pam chuckled. "You deserve a bit of spoiling. I looked in a couple of times earlier but you were sleeping like a log."

"I feel like one, Mum. Thanks, this is lovely. How's Marmalade?"

"Fine. No windgalls, sprains or cuts. She's in the paddock with Sonata, no doubt greatly exaggerating her exploits."

"Mum, you're as daft about her as I am." Jess laughed.

"I hope so, darling," said Pam, pouring the tea. She put a cup carefully on the bedside table, beside the photographs of Jess with her dad, and Marmalade with her dam, then sat on the bed.

"That nice police woman, Sergeant Pollard, has just left. She wanted to talk to you but I didn't want to disturb you. She had some news, you see."

"About the horse killer? Have they caught him?"

"Well yes - and no. At first light the police went to the field to look for clues. They saw a scrap of material on the wire fence, climbed over and on the edge of the wood found the young man - half hidden in a thicket – and - he was dead."

Jess's cup was halfway to her mouth. It tipped precariously so Pam took it from her, setting it down on the tray. "I'm sorry to give you such horrible news, Jess."

Jess's face flushed and she looked hard at her dish of muesli.

"How did he die?"

"The police think he fell on his knife, having tripped over a bramble cable. They haven't come to definite conclusions... I suppose there will be an inquest."

Jess stared at her. "Shall I have to go, Mum?"

"I don't know. I didn't think to ask Sergeant Pollard. I hope not."

"I wouldn't mind. D'you think I was the last person to see him alive? It's rather a creepy thought."

Pam squeezed her arm and smiled her most reassuring smile. Jess felt irritated that Pam expected her to be upset.

"He was an evil person, Mum; he caused his own death, didn't he?"

"Well - yes, that's true."

"Do the police know much about him, Mum?"

"Not much. He lived in digs about four miles away. He was sacked from an abattoir a few months ago, and you were right about his hobby..."

"Weight lifting?"

"Karate. He was an expert; belonged to a club in Guildford."

"So we were on the right track."

"Yes, even to his not having a car. He walked, or rode a bike."

"D'you think the police took any notice of our letter?"

"I don't know. It wouldn't be an easy thing to admit, would it? Especially if they thought people were being critical of them."

Jess finished her tea and started on the toast. Pam poured second cups.

"Oh, I nearly forgot. Mrs Selwood rang just before Sergeant Pollard arrived. She was so concerned about you - and Marmalade. She's such a kind person."

"Did she mention the foal? Is it all right?"

"Yes, it's been stitched and put on an antibiotic. The groom, Ronnie, thinks the dam put up a fight. She's quite a touchy mare anyway, and exceptionally protective of her first foal. Bill Selwood agrees, and thinks the man climbed over the fence to escape. The new Lord Connor knows all about it from both of them, and the police had to contact him about - the body - being in his wood. He'll be ringing, or writing to you."

Jess looked horrified. "Mum, he'll know I was trespassing!"

Pam laughed. "The least of his worries. He's worked it out that if the man had not died, the description you gave, and your drawing would have been sufficient evidence for a prosecution. He regards you as a heroine. And he told Mr Selwood that he felt really bad about you having to jump the gate. You could have been hurt, or worse; and *he* had given the order to have the gates padlocked!"

Jess gave a huge sigh of relief. She put out a hand and turned Pam's watch face towards her. "Crikey, I must get up. I've so much to do this week."

Pam took a watch out of her pocket and handed it to her.

"Yours, I think. It was by the soap dish in the downstairs loo."

Jess grinned, thinking of the sequence of dramatic events that might not have happened if she had been aware of the time!

"Darling, you stay in bed – rest for as long as you like," Pam advised.

"Maybe I won't ride," Jess conceded, "but I must do my tack... Oh brill, the others will be back tomorrow. I can't wait to see them.

On Tuesday, at four-ten p.m.the twins arrived home from their holiday with their grandmother, and by five they were racing down The Elms' drive on their skateboards. Then Alison turned up on her bike and, minutes later, newspapers were strewn over the kitchen table.

"Listen to this," cried Susan. "*Dangerous mission accomplished!* That's the headline, then, *Horse killer's activities curtailed by plucky schoolgirl.* Oh gosh, it goes on and on."

"It isn't even true," Jess protested, blushing. "He stopped himself by falling."

"What about this one," said Adam. "*Marvellous Marmalade* and a picture of Jess with her arms around Marmalade's neck looking really - soppy."

"I didn't want them to take it. They wanted to photograph me jumping a gate and when I wouldn't they took that silly one."

"I think it's rather sweet," said Alison, grinning, and dodged being swiped by a paper.

"We heard about it on the eight o'clock news at granny's," Susan told her.

"Same here," said Alison. "At least Mum did, then woke me to tell me all about it. I tried to ring, Jess, but the line was always engaged."

"Even Mrs Bradshaw rang." Jess said. "After saying, `Well done', she ticked me off for riding in the woods and jumping alone. I had to remember I was a Pony Club member and not to let the side down."

"Cheek," said Adam. "What about the heir to Lord Connor, does he know what happened?"

"Yes, he rang yesterday and thanked me and Marmalade. He actually said he was sorry the gate was locked, and I'd had to take such a risk jumping it. Then he said there were advantages to having watchful, responsible riders in the woods and he'd have to think again. And he wants me to decide on a present and let him know."

"What d'you think it will be?" asked Adam.

Jess grinned. "A promise that the paths will be proper bridle-ways."

"Jess! D'you think he'll agree?"

"I don't know. It's worth a try."

"Well, if he does you should be made an Honorary Life Member of the Pony Club, or given the Freedom of the Woods."

Quickly trying to outdo her brother, Susan suggested a new honour should be invented, called 'The Order of Merit and Marmalade'.

Alison gave a sudden shriek and collapsed on a chair, wiping her eyes with the back of her hand. "L - look at that..." she gasped, pushing a paper towards Adam.

"Oh no!" he started to shake with laughter, then quoted, *"When is M... M... Marmalade NOT in a jam?"*

Jess took the paper and she and Susan were instantly reduced to a state of helplessness.

"That's the Guardian," gasped Susan eventually. "Golly, Marmalade in national newspapers!"

"Why are you all crying?" asked Pam from the doorway. "Mrs Carey wants to see you all. Perhaps she'll be able to cheer you up!"

Jess awoke in a state of panic. Only one day left before the One Day Event and so much to do. She raced to the bathroom, then back to her room to pull on jeans and a tee-shirt and was downstairs as the kitchen clock struck the hour.

"Oh no, it's only seven o'clock!" she wailed aloud. She could have had another hour in bed. She filled the kettle, put bread in the toaster and switched on the radio.

"The twenty-two year old man was formally identified by a mother who had not seen her son for six years. Plucky schoolgirl, Jessica Redman, who galloped flat out and jumped a five bar gate to summon help, was the last person to..."

Jess silenced the newsreader in mid-flow. She sat down heavily, suddenly tired and close to tears. It was all getting too much for her. Anyone would have done what she did - or would they? Would her friends have risked their ponies' necks jumping that gate? Would they have panicked, galloping madly away as she had with little sense of direction?

She was still feeling fragile when Pam appeared in her dressing-gown.

"Darling, I was hoping you'd have a lie-in. Are you all right?"

"Yes thanks."

"You don't sound it."

Silently, Jess poured tea for her mother then put more bread in the toaster.

"I'm - just feeling - a bit ashamed, that's all."

"Ashamed? Why? I don't understand..."

"Well, it was Mrs Bradshaw really. I mean, saying 'Well done' and everything, then reminding me I shouldn't have been in the wood, and certainly not jumping alone."

"Oh, I see but sometimes a wrong turns into a right."

"Not really, Mum, not in this case. It was just chance I stayed late and came across the... I mean, I didn't stop the attack. If anyone did it was the mare. And I did risk Marmalade's life, didn't I?"

"You took a risk for both of you because it seemed the only way. No one has a right to criticise what you did, not knowing how it felt to be threatened in such a way. I agree you shouldn't have been there, but I know you'll never go off jumping alone again."

"But I didn't stop anything, Mum. If I hadn't been there the mare would still have defended herself and her foal, and the stupid man would still have fallen on his knife. End of dreadful story."

"And if he hadn't, or if he'd just been hurt you would have had evidence to have him arrested and no doubt convicted. End of slightly less awful story!"

Jess stared hard at the grain in the kitchen table.

"And another thing, Mum, I don't feel awful that it ended this way. I don't care about the man."

With effort she met Pam's eyes for a second, then looking away, and out of the window, she continued, "That's really wicked isn't it?"

Pam considered her question, then getting up and putting an arm around her shoulders, said, "At your age, Jess, I'd have felt just as you do. I would have seen it as rough justice. Only, when you get older you see things a bit differently. I don't mean you're not upset and angry, but you wonder why such awful things are done - what's made the person behave so cruelly, or so wickedly?"

"You mean, did he have a drunken father who beat him - or a mum who didn't love him...?" There was a note of exasperation in Jess's voice.

"Yes, that sort of thing. Some people have terrible lives."

"I don't think it's any excuse." Jess's voice was both angry and tearful now."

"Not an excuse... Never an excuse - maybe a reason," said Pam gently.

Jess scrabbled in her pocket for a tissue. "There's something else I've thought of. If God is so forgiving that awful man might meet Daddy... I don't w... want him to have to meet him..."

Giving her a hug and handing her a piece of kitchen towel, Pam said in a voice that was half-laughing and half-crying, "I wouldn't want to be in the horse killer's shoes, would you, Jess? I wouldn't rate his chances."

Two hours later Adam arrived on his skateboard, carrying a DVD. Jess glanced up from rubbing Marmalade's forelegs with her bath towel.

"Hi - come to help?"

"No," said Adam hastily. "I've got a skateboard DVD I promised to lend Mrs Carey."

Pam appeared carrying a basket of washing and overheard. Jess grinned at her and suggested Mrs Carey should only watch it if it carried a Government Health Warning.

Pam laughed. "I see your point but even Mrs Carey has to draw the line. Still, today we're off on a harmless venture to look at a telescope advertised in the local paper."

"A telescope," exclaimed Adam. "Whatever for?"

"For looking at the stars, Adam," said Jess with exaggerated slowness.

Adam grinned. "Not bad for a plucky schoolgirl," he said, parking his skateboard against the stable wall.

"It all stemmed from something Jess said," explained Pam. "Some comment about the view of the night sky through Mrs Carey's huge west window reminding her of the London Planetarium. Mrs Carey's never been there, and has always wanted to study astronomy, which is why we're off to look at this telescope."

She went away to hang out the washing and Jess trickled warm water onto Marmalade's tail from a hose, attached to the kitchen tap through the open window.

"I left Susan washing Tara so I'd better get back to start Pie, though why for a One Day Event I can't imagine. It's not as if it's a Show."

"I've had a ghastly thought, Adam," said Jess suddenly. "If Mum is gallivanting with Mrs Carey when am I going to be able to walk the course? Sally says it's quite different from the one you rode over when you were little."

"No hass," said Adam, airily, then, remembering the other reason for his visit added, "Mum said we'll pick you up about two and all walk the course together. And, Jess, you mustn't worry – a pony that can jump a five bar gate can jump anything."

Chapter 13

Although the Berrywood horsebox and the Barnes's trailer arrived in good time there were already lines and lines of boxes and trailers. Jess's confidence started to ebb and was not helped by acquaintances swooping on her with cries of, "Jolly well done," or "We heard all about you" or "It was you in the papers wasn't it?"

Two of Sally's young pupils were preparing for the minimus class, helped by a B.H.S. student called Annie. Robin, aged seven, was trying to girth up the bright, chestnut Shetland, Will-the-Bard, while his nine-year-old sister, Alice, was at the hoof oiling stage with the roan, Bandit.

"Breave in, Bardy," commanded Robin, shrilly, but the pony inflated like a bullfrog setting everyone giggling.

Jess looked at the younger children enviously; they were so calm and matter-of-fact. Once they were off towards their collecting ring, pandemonium seemed to break loose for the others. Frenzied grooming and tacking up and the usual brief arguments about the whereabouts of brushes, hoof oil, brushing boots and so on occupied half an hour.

An announcement over the relay system informed them that the overnight rainfall had slightly improved the going, and sawdust would do the rest. Fence judges were asked to meet with Mrs Trotman immediately for briefing, and the first minimus rider was expected to be on the course by ten-forty five.

"Gosh, I hope old Trotters won't terrify Granny?" Alison giggled.

"Can't imagine it," said Susan. "She's with Pam judging the water jump. She'll be okay."

"Is she standing in for your mum, Allie?" asked Sally.

"Yes, she's been in court all week. She's exhausted."

"There are always two judges at the water," Adam informed them. "One of them has to be a qualified life-saver."

"Rubbish," said Susan.

"Are you sure?" Jess asked.

"You're kidding," accused Alison.

"Yes, he is," said Sally, firmly. "The water is only a foot deep."

"Oh dear, one of Tara's plaits is coming undone," said Susan.

"I'll see to it," Sally offered.

"Oh gosh, should I have plaited?" asked Jess, feeling desperately outclassed.

"Shouldn't think it's possible, is it?" Sally looked at Marmalade's shiny, wayward mane.

"It would look far worse plaited," said Susan frankly. "Anyway, I've seen horses unplaited at Goodwood."

"It's so obvious she's not meant to be plaited," said Sally, trying to reassure Jess. "You may be overlooked for the Turnout prize, but that's not included in the score and is only for our branch. She looks beautifully clean and healthy - that's what really matters."

"Doesn't Linus look different?" enthused Adam. "He's really filled out."

"Yes, he's a changed pony," Sally agreed, "and Alison has a real partnership with him."

"Sally, if they make us show jump before the dressage we'll be wrongly dressed." Susan sounded less confident than usual.

"No you won't. You can wear a jacket for the jumping as well as for dressage then you can wear Club sweatshirts for the cross-country. And don't forget back protectors. You don't do dressage in brushing or over-reach boots, or martingales - luckily you all use snaffles, correct for this level. I'll be writing for a dressage judge so you'll have to help one another."

"I'm ready to start riding in," said Alison. "Does anyone mind if I go?"

"No," Sally answered for all of them. "Linus needs lots of working in."

Marmalade had never been so tiresome. She would not stand still in spite of being tied up next to Pie who was as calm as ever.

"Stand still you bad girl," scolded Jess, spilling hoof oil.

Sally swiftly picked up her nearside forefoot so she had to keep still, balancing on three legs.

"Gosh, thanks," said Jess.

"Would you like to borrow a surcingle?" Sally offered, seeing Jess was using only her usual girth. "It's not obligatory but a good habit to use one."

Jess accepted gratefully, wondering how she would have coped without Sally's help. She was so calm and efficient.

"Where's Mum?" asked Adam. "She just dumped us and disappeared."

"She'll be talking to all her cronies; you know what she's like at these things, it's partly nerves."

At last everyone was ready except for Adam, who was fumbling with his number tapes.

"You'll find it easier if you remove your gloves," advised Susan, with a tinge of sarcasm.

The moment Jess and Marmalade were trotting across the field they both settled down, and pony listened to rider instead of whinnying to all and sundry. They met Alison riding circles and looking boot-faced.

"I've just seen that awful Wadham-Smith woman," she said, not lowering her voice. "She stared at Linus, then said, 'Oh, that's the pony my children learnt to ride on years ago'. I didn't bother to enlighten her."

"Where is she? Can you see her?" asked Jess.

Alison looked around. "There she is, the big woman with piled-up yellow hair and wearing a scarlet bell tent."

Jess giggled. It was a most apt description.

They rode off in different directions to concentrate on riding circles and changes of rein. An announcement informed them that the first minimus rider was on the course and juniors could do their show jumping. Jess had popped Marmalade over the practice fence and looked critically at the show jumps, deciding they were quite small. She made a snap decision.

"Jolly good," beamed the steward. "We're hoping to get through all the juniors this morning. Shall I hold your pony while you walk the course?"

The jumps were clearly numbered and there was only one tight change of direction. Jess pulled her stirrups up a hole and circled, heard the starting bell, and was away. There was only one tricky moment, when Marmalade turned rather wide but they were clear at all nine jumps.

"Well done," called the steward as Jess rode by, patting and praising Marmalade.

"Brilliant," enthused Adam, who went in next and did an easy clear round.

Susan then followed suit with Tara.

"Great, all of us clear," she said. "Ali's going to do her dressage first. She thinks Linus needs to concentrate on one thing at a time. I've just seen Mum. She's helping with the scoring which she hates. She said the ghastly Wadham-Smith accosted her telling her she'd seen Ali's mum's name in the paper again, defending some n'er-do-well, as she put it. She said she couldn't understand why she wastes time with such people who are a drain on society..."

"That's typical of her sort," interrupted Adam.

"I hadn't finished," said Susan, crossly. "She then said that Ali's Mum, being a lone parent, had a duty to make money and send her daughter to a decent school and she wouldn't do that fighting for lost causes."

"That's terribly rude!" exclaimed Jess. "She must know you both go to the same school as Ali."

"Oh, she does, but she doesn't care."

"Why is she particularly nasty to Ali?" asked Jess, watching Pam and Ali's grandmother trying to indicate the right route to a small rider, without undue interference.

"Mum says it's professional jealousy. Mr W-H is a country solicitor doing really boring things to do with selling houses; the only time he got his name in the paper was when he denied his dog had killed someone's pet rabbit and was taken to court and fined."

"Gosh, how embarrassing for him," said Jess, laughing.

"Don't say anything to Ali, will you, she might get upset just as she's about to compete."

"Susan, as if I would," Jess said, indignantly. "Here she comes."

"Did you see me?" called Alison.

"No, why?"

"I've done my test. It wasn't too bad. At least I remembered it. I'll do the jumping now, once I've put my back protector on on. Have you been round?"

"Yes, we all went clear," Susan replied. "You'll be okay."

And she was. Linus made no attempt to stop or run out and loped round with an expression of nonchalance, or so Adam said.

"Now for your tests," said Alison. "I think you're first, Jess."

Slowly riding to the arena, Jess muttered the test to herself. She gave her number to the steward then rode quietly about letting Marmalade have a good look at the white boards until summoned to begin. She took a deep breath, looked straight ahead and they trotted up to X. with a confident air. As if a CD had switched itself on in her brain, she was hearing her own voice telling her the next movement.

"She's going well. Marmalade is so responsive and accurate," enthused Alison.

"You'd never believe it's their first test," Adam responded.

"I can't fault her," admitted Susan."They're amazing. Look at those smooth transitions - and Jess always says she's hopeless at canter!"

Beaming with relief, Jess rode towards them. "I nearly forgot to walk on a loose reign," she called.

"Well, it didn't show," Adam said. "You were brilliant."

"Terrific," added Alison.

Tara and Susan had just started their test; so they watched from a sensible distance so as not to distract them. The only fault they could find was that Tara was a bit strong in canter which spoilt her last downward transition.

In went Adam and Pie and performed a reasonable test but it was lacking in enthusiasm, and Pie was a bit late going into canter.

"They really don't enjoy dressage much and it shows," observed Susan.

Adam returned, making much of Pie and saying the worst was over.

"Not for me," said Jess.

"Nor me," agreed Alison. "Still, we've only one thing left to think about."

They put head collars over bridles and tied the ponies up while they pulled on Pony Club sweatshirt and tie-on number tabards.

"I hate my protector. More like a straight jacket," complained Jess. Hers was new and stiff as a board.

"Must've been awful riding in armour," suggested Alison, already pink in the face. "Thank goodness it's a bit cooler today."

They helped each other

"Boots!" exclaimed Susan.

"Oh no!" responded Jess, "I don't think I can bend down now."

With much giggling they accomplished the feat of fastening on brushing boots, thanking Heaven for Velcro, then Tara and Linus had to have martingales fitted. They had just finished when the fence judges were asked to change the flags, and the juniors were told they would be starting in five minutes.

"I can't..." Adam thrust Pie's reins at Susan. "I must go to the loo. Bring Pie over, will you?" He dashed off.

"Come on Pie, there's a good chap. That's his second trip to the loo. It's nerves of course - not for himself but for his beloved Pie."

"Can we decide our own order or will they call numbers?" enquired Jess, anxiously.

As if in reply the commentator called the first ten numbers.

"That's Susan and Adam," said Alison.

Adam tore back down the slope and took hold of Pie.

"Good luck," they all called as Susan rode to the start.

They watched intently as Tara cleared all the visible jumps with ease, then disappeared into the next field. By then Adam had started and was going equally well. Over the public address system they learnt that Susan was still clear and negotiating the gate.

"Is the gate in the timed section?" Jess asked, urgently. "I can't remember."

"Yes, and the previous three jumps."

"Our eighth competitor has started; so will the following please be ready..."

"That's us," said Alison. "You're first Jess. Good luck, you'll be okay."

Waiting for the starting signal Jess felt sick with nerves, then they were off and, within seconds, she knew it was going to be all right. Determination overcame fear, and, after flying the fallen tree, the tyres and the palisade, she found she was enjoying herself. Up the slight incline and through the gateway and they were into the timed section. With the brush fence and the log pile behind them, they approached the tiger trap in the hedge with iron determination. Neither of them had jumped one before but they were over and into the third field, turning on sixpence to check, open and negotiate the hunting gate, then streak uphill to the quarry. Here

Marmalade steadied for a slight drop, then tucked her hocks under her for the jump out over a sloping hurdle.

No need to hurry, Jess thought, as they turned in a wide arc to start the descent to a sloping fence that she no longer dreaded. A burst of energy took them safely onto the wide bank, with Jess remembering to clutch a handful of mane and thank Heaven for the practice in the woods. Next the combination, then a controlled downhill approach to the mini lake. With a fleeting grin in Pam's direction she was through and heading for the final jump. Even now she could take no chances. Marmalade had not met blue-painted oil drums before, and now was not the time to stop and get to know them!

With legs clamped on like a vice, Jess cried, "Over Marmalade!" and they were.

"What a round! What a round!" cried the delighted commentator. "Jessica Redman on the 12.2 Exmoor, Marmalade. They've had rather a lot of publicity lately, so I'll say no more except brilliantly well done!"

There were laughs and cheers. Jess leapt off to hug Marmalade, then Adam, Pie, Susan and Tara.

"Look, Ali's coming down to the water," cried Adam, "and she's clear so far."

Chapter 14

Linus was trotting down the slope, to be steadied by Alison then ridden strongly to the bank. He stopped! The twins and Jess groaned. Linus changed his mind and took an enormous, unconsidered leap. Alison was ejected into the air; seemed to be returning to the saddle but at the crucial moment Linus was not there. She landed in the lake in a neat, sitting position, sending up a fountain of water that blurred everyone's vision. There were gasps of concern and horror. The St. John's ambulance's engine started up and, for once, the commentator was lost for words.

The picture cleared; the concern turned to relief and approval, then enthusiastic applause. Staggering to her feet, spluttering and almost helpless with laughter, Alison waded towards Linus who glanced at her, slightly abashed, then lowered his head to drink.

The fence judges, concerned grandmother and qualified nurse, could be heard over the public address system nearly crying with laughter.

Alison removed duckweed from the brim of her hat, found Linus's reins and mounted, water pouring off her as she squelched into the saddle. Adam, Susan and Jess were leaning weakly against their ponies, incapable of speech. Alison and Linus jumped the nasty blue drums together, to deafening cheers and the wholehearted admiration of riders, spectators and officials alike.

Back at the box Adam took care of Linus while Alison rummaged inside for dry clothes.

"Good thing I brought old togs," she called, throwing her dripping jodhpurs and sweatshirt over the partition. She emerged wearing grooming overalls and rubbing her hair with Linus's day sheet.

A forty-five minute break was announced and fence judges left their posts. Pam and Jane Scott, Alison's grandmother, arrived with Lin who said she was very sorry to have missed the aqua show.

"Gran, you haven't even asked if I'm all right," said Alison, tipping water out of her jodhpur boots.

"I can see you're all right, darling, but my nerves are in shreds."

"I shall keel over if we don't eat soon," grumbled Adam.

"You're disgusting, Adam," said Susan. "You'll get too heavy for Pie if you don't stop eating."

Adam grinned, good-humoured as ever.

"I could do a swop with Jess. She says Exmoors can carry a grown man with ease."

"D'you know at least two famous racehorses had some Exmoor blood," Alison told them. "One of them won the Grand National."

Lunchtime was hilarious .The grown-ups drank ice cold lager which,

Adam complained was not adequate for the occasion. He ate four giant sandwiches, two chicken drumsticks, three packets of crisps and an apple, washed down with two cans of coke.

"Mum, you should stop him. He's obsessed with food."

"Could be worse," said Lin, philosophically. "Strange, he's not even tubby but, the next time we worm the dogs, we'd better include Adam."

Robin and Alice also had huge appetites. Their mother had been unable to get the day off from her work but they were unperturbed to be without her.

"Why do little children always talk at the tops of their voices?" Jess asked Alison in an undertone.

Alison giggled. "It's awful, isn't it? I should think our hearing is at serious risk."

Both the younger ones had completed each phase of their competition, although Robin had fallen off at a cross-country fence. Seeing him unconcernedly trying to remount on the off-side, which was annoying his pony, the fence judge had bunked him up, hoping everyone would be kind and turn a blind eye.

Sally took a slice of quiche from the huge, pooled picnic, and said she was thinking of hiring out Linus and Ali for film stunt work, which started them all laughing again. Lin said Ali's name would be preserved in the Pony Club archives.

"And Horse and Hound will want to do a centre-page spread," suggested Pam. "Probably provided by Jess's friend from the Advertiser who was snapping away like mad."

"Glad it's not us this afternoon," said Susan, squinting against the sunlight.

"Tom's riding in the seniors," said Jess, reading the programme. "Why is that?"

"He's riding his mother's cob which is above the juniors' height limit," Sally explained. "We had to introduce a limit when children started competing on their parents' huge hunters."

"Good job there isn't a lower height limit," commented Jess.

"Yes," said Sally, "especially as Marmalade is capable of jumping the seniors' fences."

Jess smiled. "I see the older Wadham-Smith's entered," she said.

"That'll be worth a laugh," said Adam.

"The younger one went clear," Jane told them, "but was so slow she was overtaken by two others."

"I don't think that pony's well," Sally said. "Looks really tucked up."

"Ugh, something's trickling down my neck," screeched Jess. "It's icy."

"It's slimy water running off Ali's back protector. I put it on the trailer roof to dry," admitted Adam. He glanced at his watch. "You fence judges had better sober up, you're on in ten minutes. Is your watch still working, Ali?"

She grinned. "Of course, serious eventers all wear waterproof watches. I'm surprised you don't know that, Adam."

Present, if not very correct the fence judges took up their positions and Adam and Susan saddled up to be score collectors for the senior class. Alison and Jess scrambled onto the roof of the Berrywood box for a grandstand view.

"The elder W-S has started and the horse is going quite well, although she's hanging onto its mouth," Alison said.

"Must be a courageous horse then," Jess replied, shading her eyes to follow its progress.

"It is and it's wasted on Olivia. Gosh, she's fallen off. Look - at the brush. All the horse did was jump! The poor thing's even waiting for her."

Jess giggled. "Maybe it's a glutton for punishment as Maggie would say."

The fence judge had blown her whistle to delay the next competitor, which was going to create confusion later as the fall had happened in the timed section. She was about to wave the red flag when Olivia got up and walked to her horse.

"Could the ambulance go to fence seven, please? No, not the fence judge - it's the mother insisting - ridiculous ..."

Alison and Jess exchange delighted grins.

"We weren't meant to hear that; he should have switched off. Oh, look Jess, she's trying to mount although the ambulance is roaring up."

There then followed quite a pantomime. Mrs Wadham-Smith got out of the ambulance with a first-aider and both hurried to Olivia, who was tightening the girth. There was a lot of arm waving and shouting between mother and daughter, during which the embarrassed first-aider sidled away and drove back to base. Walking beside the horse, still arguing with Olivia, Mrs Wadham-Smith was unconcerned that they were in the way of oncoming riders.

"Do I take it that competitor 108 has retired? If so, could the course be cleared? Perhaps we can now get on..."

Jess and Alison screeched with laughter.

"He didn't exactly hide his feelings, did he?" gasped Alison. "Oh look, Tom's going brilliantly, and Jane Parker's just finished and was clear. She's one of ours. Her parents have the village shop at Down Berry. Her mare is gorgeous. And she always wins the Best Turned Out rosette."

Once the last competitor had finished, a break of thirty minutes was announced before prize-giving.

"Let's see if our dressage marks are up," suggested Alison.

It was not possible to get near the scoreboards for the crush of competitors but Alison's hawk-like eyes picked out Jess's name and Susan's.

"Jess, you got a 58, that's better than Susan, and she was second last year. Oh gosh though, is it high score good or bad? Usually they add up the penalties so it's low score good. D'you see what I mean?"

"No," replied Jess, utterly confused.

"Well, let's find the others, I expect they'll know."

Adam and Susan were putting the ponies in the trailer.

"Jess has a 58 for dressage," cried Alison, "is that okay?"

"Okay! It's brilliant. Did you see ours?" asked Susan.

"Only yours which was 69. So low score is good?"

"Depends how they are doing it," said Adam. "I'd say a 58 was pretty good for a plucky schoolgirl, wouldn't you, Susan?"

"Oh, shut up, Adam," said Jess, her nerves in a very taut state.

"Did you see the Wadham-Smith fiasco?" asked Alison.

Susan laughed. "Saw it and heard it. Mrs W-S blamed the fence judge, the course owner, the commentator, the British Horse Society and the poor horse. She'll probably sue them all."

"But Olivia simply fell off! We had a marvellous view from the lorry roof."

"No, mai dear, she was viciously thrown. Her delicate sensibilities are seriously damaged. She may nevah, nevah ride again."

"What an appalling loss to the equestrian world," said Adam. "I say, is there time for tea?"

"Definitely not," said Sally, suddenly appearing. "Prize-giving is about to start. Come on, we don't want to miss any of it."

After thanking all the organisers and helpers, Mrs Bradshaw began to read the results. Loud cheers acclaimed every placing but even louder and longer ones when it was a branch member. Highest placed member in the minimus class was Amanda Cobb who was fourth overall, but every child competing had a rosette. Tension mounted as Mrs Bradshaw picked up the junior list.

"Starting in sixth place..." The children listened but did not hear, until, "And in fourth place Susan Barnes and Tara."

There was a long delay for the clapping and cheering to die down. Third and second places went to members of other branches, then, pausing to adjust her spectacles and beam around in a maddeningly slow way, Mrs Bradshaw announced, "First overall - so first also for the branch - Jessica Redman and Marmalade."

Her words were drowned after the first syllable. With a push from Adam, Jess stepped forward, with the others to collect her prize to loud clapping and cheering.

When the branch results followed Jess registered delightedly that Adam and Pie were fifth and Susan and Tara second. Collecting the branch cup and rosette she was acutely embarrassed to be hugged by Mrs Bradshaw, who said, "Marmalade was a heroine last Sunday, and she is again today. She is only 12.2 yet her speed was unbeaten and her dressage score the highest of the first two classes."

Scarlet-faced but nearly bursting with pride in her pony, Jess returned to the others.

"Before we go on to the seniors' results I have great pleasure in presenting a special rosette for good sportsmanship. It was suggested by our commentator, Mr Anderson, and endorsed by many others. Alison, for your aquatic display and the wonderful way you coped with it!" Mrs Bradshaw handed her a huge, multi-coloured rosette to an explosion of clapping, wolf whistles and cheering.

Struggling in their excitement to concentrate on the senior placings, they only registered that Jane Parker was first overall, and Tom was third.

A visiting District Commissioner complimented the host branch for an excellent event and profusely thanked all the organisers and helpers.

"I think you and Marmalade were wonderful," said a familiar voice, and Jess turned in surprise to find Annette Wadham-Smith at her side.

"Oh, thanks. Your pony went clear didn't he?"

"Yes, but he was very slow."

"I'd get his teeth checked and, perhaps, a blood test. Shall I have a word with your mother?" said Sally, standing alongside Jess.

"She's gone," Annette replied, miserably. "She loaded up and went home to drop the ponies off, then take Olivia to the hospital, which is crazy. She's forgotten all about me. I don't know how I'm going to get home."

"No problem," said Sally, decisively. "You come with us, we'll see you get home."

Walking to the box lines, led by Annie with Robin and Alice dancing alongside proudly flourishing their rosettes, Annette told the children that she hated her sister and her mother.

"I expect she was upset and just didn't think," suggested Susan, although privately shocked by Mrs Wadham-Smith's behaviour.

"She didn't forget, she just doesn't care. As long as her darling Olivia is all right that's all that matters."

Unable to believe their ears the others heard Susan say, "Come and ride with us sometime. We have a really good time."

"I've often wanted to, but Olivia always decides what we do and where we go. Maybe, if she gives up riding, I'll be able to."

Adam nudged Jess. "Has Susan gone mad?"

"Ssh... I think Annette could be quite nice. We ought to give her a chance," Jess replied, surprising herself.

The newly acquired telescope was positioned in the alcove pointing upwards through the west window. Much as she longed to try it, Jess was absorbed with giving Mrs Carey a detailed and vivid account of the day.

"Dear, wonderful Marmalade. And so you are now in the One Day Event team - all of you."

"Yes, all of us. Ali would have tied in sixth place if she hadn't fallen off."

"Well, I think you are all wonderful. I do hope there'll be lots of photographs."

"I doubt if Jane Scott and I will ever be asked to fence judge again," said Pam from the sofa by the window. "I'm afraid we didn't behave very responsibly."

"Ah, but Alison wasn't hurt. You behaved appropriately for the occasion, just as you did the day Sam collapsed. That reminds me - I haven't told Jess our good news."

"Gosh, what more can there be? So many nice things have happened lately."

But before Mrs Carey could continue her telephone rang. She answered it reluctantly but, within seconds, was smiling happily as she handed the receiver to Jess. "For you, dear - Mrs Bradshaw."

"Jess, wonderful news! The new Lord Connor has informed The County Council that he wants the paths in his woods to become official bridle-ways. The local B.H.S. bridle-ways officer called here earlier with a copy of the letter, and I can't imagine they will refuse such a request."

"Gosh no. That's brilliant. Thank you for ringing me."

"Not at all. We should all be thanking you."

After a few more compliments Mrs Bradshaw rang off, and Jess imparted he r news. When the excitement had lessened a little, Jess reminded Mrs Carey that she'd been on the verge of making an announcement.

"Yes, Sam is coming home. He'll have all sorts of aids and gadgets to help him. Jenny will let her house in London to some friends and live here with him. She really wants to live in the country again. I'm hoping, in time, Sam will be able to cope with a motorised wheelchair - I've sent for details."

Jess was amazed and delighted, but for a fleeting moment she had a vision of Sam whizzing up the garden path to inspect her stable management. Smiling, she sprawled on the end of Mrs Carey's bed and looked around the room that she still found beautiful. In pride of place, right in the middle of the many photographs, hung one of her sketches. It showed Sonata, watched by Marmalade, rolling in the paddock; a landmark in her progress, exciting as a toddler's first steps!

Suddenly, Jess said, "The time's flown since we came here. It's strange, isn't Mum, that things are now so different. I thought we'd always see ourselves as exiles from the moor."

Chapter 15

September was a glorious month. After much-needed rain, hated by holidaymakers and welcomed by riders, the refreshed trees held on to their leaves and the grass revived, causing sensible owners to watch their ponies' girths and for early signs of laminitis. Marmalade was not pleased to spend hours in the stable when there was a considerable amount of mowing to be done.

Standing at the ropes at the one hundredth anniversary of the County Show, Adam and Susan wished they'd anticipated better going, and had entered their ponies for a Working Hunter Pony Class, before the entries closed weeks ago. They were, however, largely compensated by Marmalade surviving the preliminary judging that morning (an unprecedented measure to cope with the excessive number of entries), and she was now walking around with eleven other finalists in the Novice Mixed Mountain and Moorland Class for small breeds.

Alison, who was helping Sally, dashed across to watch in between leading horses back from the young stock classes, putting the finishing touches to Sally's beautiful hunter, and assisting with a Top Secret Venture - soon to be revealed.

Jess, Adam, and Susan had got up at dawn to prepare Marmalade for her début in the show ring. She and Jess had stayed overnight with the Barnes family and Lin had driven them to the show in the trailer. The twins now felt a considerable amount of personal pride and satisfaction as they admired Marmalade's presentation.

"That's a lovely pony," said a stud owner standing nearby. "I can't get over the numbers and quality of Exmoors this year. There were five in this mornings round and three have got through to this afternoon."

Her companion said it was most unusual to see so many, but it was not a breed that had ever attracted her. If she was aware of two pairs of hostile eyes giving her 'looks to kill', she gave no sign. She sounded Welsh and there were more Welsh Section A's in this class than any other breed.

"I love that little brown Dartmoor," enthused Adam. "What an amazing shoulder."

"Almost as nice as Marmalade," said Susan, loyally, "but I agree she moves beautifully."

The preliminary line-up had the twins gripping each other in excitement. At the top was a Welsh Section A stallion, then a Welsh mare, followed by the eye-catching Dartmoor, a Shetland, another Dartmoor, then Marmalade. The twins did not seriously look at the other six ponies.

The stallion's individual show was superb and wholly professional, the mare was well-behaved, and the little Dartmoor received a spontaneous burst of applause. The Shetland shocked everyone by bucking at canter, almost dislodging his jockey, and the second Dartmoor behaved well but struck off on the wrong leg which the rider appeared not to notice.

Marmalade stepped out of line eagerly and stood looking very proud as the judge walked all around her. She moved off at the lightest touch from Jess and her transitions were perfectly smooth. Her circles on either rein had just the right amount of bend. Adam winced as Susan's nails dug into his wrist but he didn't even pull away, so mesmerised was he by Marmalade's gallop, which slowed so beautifully and smoothly into canter, then trot, then walk. She stood like a rock while Jess loosed her reins and bowed to the judge.

Grinning broadly in the twins' direction, she rode back into line and dismounted. Susan picked up the grooming kit and ducked under the ropes to help Jess with the next phase, unsaddling and tidying up for the run-up in front of the judge.

"You're both looking terrific," she whispered.

"She's absolutely full of herself," said Jess breathlessly. "She could buck or something if we canter again."

The remainder of the individual and the in-hand shows seemed to take for ever. All Jess's practising proved worthwhile and her performance was very polished. Not all the exhibitors had paid enough attention to this part of the show and several ponies hung back, swung out badly as they turned, and one tried to tow its owner back to the collecting ring.

Saddles back on, stable rubbers passed swiftly over foamy bit rings, and jockeys aloft again, the helpers left the ring for the final ride round.

Watching intently and totally absorbed, Susan had a sudden uncanny feeling that she knew what the judge wanted. Did she have the beginnings of an 'eye' for judging? She knew the Welsh stallion would hold his place and the Welsh mare would not. Predictably the lovely Dartmoor mare moved into second place. The judge's eyes followed the walking ponies. Susan stopped breathing. Adam felt faint. The steward moved towards Marmalade. Susan closed her eyes and when she opened them again Marmalade was standing in third place. She hugged Adam, who didn't even complain. Below Marmalade stood the other Welsh pony, moved down from second place, then came the other Dartmoor and, finally, the naughty Shetland was replaced by one standing below it. The remaining ponies, all quality animals but unlucky this time, left the ring to sympathetic clapping.

"Ladies and gentlemen, we have the results of the Novice Ridden Mountain and Moorland Class for small breeds. These ponies are four years and over, and have not yet won a first prize in a similar class. The quality of these ponies is extremely high and they represent some of our finest native pony studs. We are particularly pleased and encouraged to have had five Exmoor ponies competing, one of which is in the final placing. The Exmoor is classed as a rare breed...."

"Why doesn't he just get on with it," complained Adam.

"Don't be so rotten, Adam. It's good publicity for native breeds, especially Exmoors. They are an endangered species."

"... and the results are as follows..."

Jess had to look up the names in the catalogue much later. She heard nothing except:

"...and in third place, White Ridge Marmalade, owned and ridden by Jessica Redman; also winner of the Exmoor Pony Society Best of Breed rosette."

Vaguely aware of an unseemly dance going on outside the ropes Jess spotted her mother and Alison on the other side of the ring, waving like mad. She risked a discreet wave after the smiling judge had moved down the line.

Rosettes handed out, cups touched for a second for the benefit of the photographers, then collected later by the winners, and the six triumphant riders cantered their lap of honour.

The twins and Lin were waiting by the collecting ring to hug and congratulate them.

"Where's Mum?" Jess had lost sight of Pam.

"Don't worry, she saw you." Lin smiled. "I expect she's looking after Mrs Carey."

"D'you know she bucked as we galloped round? Trust Marmalade to wait until the rosette was safely bagged! She's so clever!"

Adam and Susan laughed happily and hugged the pony again and again, then escorted them both back to the box lines. Jess untacked, while Adam gave Marmalade a small feed, offered her water, and tied a small net of hay to the side of the trailer. Susan collected the beautiful dark blue rug with Jess's initials in the corner. It, and a blue headcollar, had been bought with some of the reward money given by Lord Connor and other horse owners.

"Too warm, I think." Susan changed her mind and put it safely in the car. "Will she be all right outside? It's very warm in the trailer."

Jess and Adam considered this.

"A bit risky," said Jess. "She won't do anything silly but someone else might."

Overhearing, a woman in the next car, said she would be around for a while and would keep on eye on her.

"Thanks, that's really kind," said Jess. "I can't imagine she'll do anything except eat."

As they walked away Marmalade lifted her head, listening intently. She began to munch, but every now and then stopped, tensed and listened, every nerve alert.

Adam looked longingly at a purple and pink hot air balloon high above them. They wandered past trade tents and Adam bought a hoof pick for Jess, who accepted it happily, not telling him she already had two. They lingered to look at the rare breeds, then Susan glanced at her watch and said they must see what was happening in the main ring.

"Probably the parade of the West Belchester hounds," suggested Jess, without enthusiasm.

The twins exchanged discreet winks. Having 'lost' the programme, Susan said they'd better go and check, in case they missed something exciting.

"Not the Motorbike Acrobats," groaned Jess. "I can't bear the noise."

"No, it won't be, but there's the Heavy Horse parade, the Dancing Diggers and all kinds of special events 'cause it's the Centenary."

Susan led them on decisively; Adam even walked past the Hot Dog caravan without hesitating. As they reached a spare three feet of rope at the main ring, an announcement was starting as if on perfect cue.

"Ladies and gentlemen, we have yet another special event. In honour of our Founders and of past Presidents, Members and Exhibitors, we have a Distinguished Veterans Parade. Each of the twelve horses has had a highly distinguished career in a variety of spheres, show jumping, showing and dressage. What they all have in common is that they were prolific and regular winners at this show. We thought it appropriate that the parade should be headed by a mare, owned and bred by a past President, the late Colonel Carey. We are delighted that Mrs Carey is with us this afternoon and, sitting beside her in the stand, is her friend and stud groom, Mr Samuel Hall."

Jess stared at the gleaming brown horse just entering the ring. Speechless, she looked wonderingly from one twin to the other then back at Sonata, ridden by a familiar figure in an unfamiliar way.

At last she recovered her powers of speech. "It's Mum! But she doesn't ride side-saddle!"

The twins were grinning broadly.

"You've known about this all along! How did you manage to keep it from me?"

"Wasn't easy," admitted Adam, with casual modesty. "It was Mrs Carey's idea. She wanted to do something really special for you and Sam. She got a firm to make a lightweight saddle, and some of the 'gallivanting' was done at Sally's. Your mum's a complete natural - the easiest person Sally's ever taught."

Transfixed, Jess watched her mother at the head of the line, elegant in a borrowed habit, and Sonata pointed her hooves and arched her neck at the poll, flexing in the gleaming double bridle as if she were young again and about to win the Ladies' Hunter Class.

A brief history was given of each horse, drawing comments from the audience, "Oh yes, I remember," and "Wembley, nineteen…What year was it?" The children learnt that Sonata had won the Ladies' Hunter Class five times, three in succession, and had bred two foals, all winning championships many times. She had been reserve champion at the Horse of the Year Show, and the Carey's had turned down an enormous sum offered by an American breeder.

"Gosh," said Jess, and the inadequacy of the response set the others giggling. "Oh look, Mrs Carey and Sam in the front of the stand - and Jenny, Maggie, and Maggie's farmer grandson…"

Jess was unaware that tears were trickling down her face and although she was holding Susan's hand in a vice-like grip, her friend did not flinch.

The commentator continued, "The sum of the ages of these horses adds up to two hundred and fifty-two years, which Mr Sam Hall tells me even beats his age."

There was a great surge of laughter, clapping and cheering and, as it died away, the audience was asked to consider the time and care spent on these veteran horses, and Adam gave Jess a meaningful nudge in the ribs. He spotted Tom Latcham and asked if they'd mind managing without him for a bit.

"Cheek!" said Susan. "We shan't see them for ages. They'll stuff themselves with disgusting food then make themselves sick at the funfair."

The twelve horses were approaching the grandstand; as they walked by Pam gently checked Sonata and turned her to face the audience. With perfect timing the eleven other riders did the same. The men raised their hats and all bowed. In the grandstand everyone, who was able, stood up and clapped and cheered. Now even Susan's cheeks were damp.

"I apologise for interrupting at this wonderful moment," began the commentator who sounded as if he were grinning broadly, "but a loose pony has joined the queue at the tea tent - the striped marquee… Oh, it's now jumped the queue - well not literally, thank goodness - and is devouring a strawberry flan. The pony is wearing a blue head collar and is said to be an Exmoor…"

Exchanging an all-comprehending look that combined horror, delight and hilarity, the girls simultaneously shrieked, "MARMALADE !!"

Lightning Source UK Ltd.
Milton Keynes UK
UKOW03f0626110414

229803UK00002B/23/P